CASEY

CASEY:
The Bi-coastal Kid

Jim Brogan

Equanimity Press
Bolinas, California

Equanimity Press
440 Aspen Road
Box 839
Bolinas, CA 94924

Cover Art: Pat Brennan
Design: David Crossman

Library of Congress Card Number 81-69478
ISBN 0-941362-01-9

PART I

COTUIT, 1989

Saturday, June, 10, 1989 Cotuit, Massachusetts

Here we go again! Back at Granny McCoy's house on Cape Cod for another summer of fun. It's time to put away my "BORED OF EDUCATION" sweatshirt until Labor Day. Boy, Dad certainly didn't wait very long to start having some fun up here. About an hour after unpacking this morning, I casually wandered into the folks' bedroom looking (honestly) for this journal. What a surprise! There were Sally and Dad lying in bed together, kissing each other, covered only by a fresh, clean, yellow sheet from their waists down.

First I was shocked, then relieved that they weren't too caught up to notice me.

They spotted me immediately. I felt like I ought to say *something*, so I blurted out, "Don't stop just because of me," while I nonchalantly extended my right hand out in front of me like an emcee presenting a famous act.

"It's just being back at Granny's summer house, Casey. It always brings out my romantic side. Yours too, Sal."

Sally nodded in agreement, but was definitely embarrassed, so I nodded my approval with a grin and started tiptoeing out quietly, but in a very exaggerated way to break the tension. Suddenly Dad threw his pillow at me, bopping me in the back of the head. That was just the excuse I needed to get the hell out of there as fast as I could.

My little intrusion on their privacy wasn't anything this household couldn't handle. The whole family has seen each other in the buff ever since I can remember. And, to tell the truth, even though she's my step-mom and in her middle forties, Sally is one, fine, attractive woman. And then there are those sweet, deep-brown, totally accepting eyes. I guess I like her so much because she never puts you down, even when she's irritable or you've done something you should feel terrible about—that's just not her style.

I remember I even had a silly crush on her in 1981, the year before she married Dad, when she was my third grade teacher and Dad was on the Board of Education in Hastings.

Those years, when I was seven and eight, when Mom and Dad were fighting about their divorce, seem now almost as if they never happened. I still love Mom a lot and I'm looking forward to spending a few weeks at her place out in California next month, but I guess Mom and Dad were just not meant to be husband and wife. It seems to be a common problem—they married in 1968 when they were both too young, right out of college. After a few years, even with the two of us little kids to care for, Mom started feeling worthless since she wasn't using any of the skills she had developed at college. She had worked in an office for three years to help Dad through law school and then she became stuck at home while he got so into his career—he's kind of a workaholic—that he had little time for her. You know, I think the more she complained, the harder he worked. It may have been a vicious circle. I even suspect he became so busy at the office because he wanted to avoid her.

Luckily, Mom's friend, Valerie, was around to help Mom, and luckily for Dad, his best friend, Pat, was still living and teaching in Hastings. Valerie and Pat both became surrogate parents for us. Then, with Val's encouragement, Mom moved out to California in 1981 in order to begin again with a "clean slate" and spent a lot of time in therapy with a woman who really helped her. After a while she met Herb, a therapist too, at a party out there in 1982. They ended up getting married about the same time as Dad and Sally. And so my sister Becky and I got to go to two weddings on two different coasts. Then Mom went to graduate school at Cal and eventually became a family counselor. Best of all, Dad and Mom became friends again, and they've hardly fought at all over the last few years.

My mind once again flashes back to the domestic bliss of Sally and Dad making love this afternoon. As a matter of fact, for me it was great seeing them so relaxed and enjoying each other so much. Dad and I are finally getting past the stage where he has to play such heavy-duty games with me. God, I've been so angry at him so much in the last few years. I couldn't stand the way *he* can't live up to what he tells us to do. Sometimes I wonder whether his way of bringing up kids is causing us to become weird.

But maybe I shouldn't blame him so much. It's a jungle of a world out there, and he's trying to do his best to help us make sense out of it. Serious Adult Life does loom ahead (far ahead, I hope.) My trip west to see Mom next month may well reveal where I'm going to spend the next four years. Sorry, Dad, no Ivy League for me. I'll have to write Danny to tell him I want to tour some colleges while I'm out there—at least Berkeley, Stanford, and Santa Cruz. Dad would love to see me try for Harvard, but there's no way I'm going to such a heavy-duty place when I'm not even sure what I want to do yet. Of course Dad's been great about it all—he's never even hinted I should be a lawyer like him (or a teacher like Sally and Pat or a therapist like Mom and Herb or like anyone.)

As for me, I know that someday I'm going to be a writer. But even if I improve a lot, I suppose I'll still have to figure out a way to make a living. Dad definitely expects *some* kind of career from me.

Saturday, June 17, 1989

This time I feel like trying to pretend I'm a novelist and writing about what happened last Sunday—so here goes:

DÉJÀ VU—WITH A TWIST

During his second day at the Cape, Casey once again sauntered into his parents' bedroom only to suffer an extreme sense of *déjà vu*. Oh no, he thought, it's Dad and Sally making love. I've intruded again.

But Casey hadn't looked quite carefully enough to draw an accurate conclusion. Yes, there was his Dad, Chuck McCoy, once again without a shirt under that same yellow sheet, right in the middle of a dreary, overcast afternoon. But the other body was definitely not Sally's. It was, in fact, male. Indeed, it was Pat who had arrived for a visit from Boston the previous evening.

Luckily the two men were apparently asleep, for they gave no signs of having noticed him. Once again Casey started to tiptoe out. Suddenly he turned around to stare at what his eyes had at first refused to register. Pat was actually holding Chuck as if his Dad were a little boy. It *was* a relief for him to realize that there didn't seem to be anything sexual about the situation. Chuck had, after all, made it clear long since that those couple of weeks with Pat during Chuck's senior year at college clearly defined the extent of his "bisexual phase".

Still, it was a shock for Casey to see Chuck, old compulsively responsible, Mr. Gray-Hair-Streaked-With-Worry, Charles McCoy, actually curled up asleep in the arms of another man. Casey stared at the scene for a minute or so and then quietly exited, relieved he had not disturbed them, for he knew his father had come up to the Cape dog-tired.

Pat was going to be around for a few days, this time without his lover, Eddie. Imagine, thought

Casey, Pat and Chuck had actually been boyhood friends, before Pat's family moved away from Hastings when they were eleven. But they had once again become best friends at college. Now, on the rare occasions when Chuck and Pat got drunk together, they would always reminisce about college days, later shifting gears and recalling the times when they'd visit each other after school and stay over at each other's houses, just as Casey and his best friend, Mark, did when they were ten and eleven.

Since then, Charles F. McCoy had become one of the most respected of those few lawyers truly interested in defending civil liberties. He was so good at it because he had learned to get along with just about every kind of person. But his heroic work for the underdog had clearly taken its toll on him. He had, according to the objective eyes of his only son, become nervous and controlling much of the time. To his credit, he had held down his blood pressure after pretty much becoming a vegetarian. Nor had he complained any more about stomach pains since he'd limited his city commutes to four days a week, although Casey wondered how he could stand even that much deadly routine.

Later that evening, while falling asleep, Casey once more let the image of Pat and Chuck in bed pop into his mind. Casey was curious about both their childhood together and that short-lived affair in college. Obviously, they still thought it was okay to be physically close. Casey guessed that Pat might be willing to return to their sexual phase, but dear old Dad had drawn up some pretty tight boundaries around his sexual identity. "You lads go ahead and do what you want to do," Casey remembered him saying, "but me, I only have enough energy for one lover, my wife, what with my kids, work, and my other responsibilities in the community. I've had to make a choice and I've chosen Sally, just Sally, and all in all I think this is what's best for me."

Casey mulled over these words and pondered his Dad's case for a bit. Funny, Chuck hadn't made any new close friendships with men since college, nobody who even came close to comparing with Pat. Although his dad claimed to hate competition and even avoided the sailboat racing in Cotuit, when it came to his career, he was still plenty competitive. But then how could he not be in the crazy world of New York City?

Even if Chuck had kept away from closeness with men, Casey still lived in an environment where it was quite difficult to avoid references to such subject matter. Indeed, he thought, I move in circles where I will keep meeting men who will dig me physically. And then Casey remembered sitting at dinner a couple of years ago when Pat remarked to Chuck and Sally how attractive Casey was becoming. Of course, as respectable parents, Chuck and Sally had registered some mock-shock, but they really didn't mind and neither did Casey. Actually, he recalled that the incident had sort of made him feel good about himself, just as he was getting into the adolescent blues and becoming very self-critical about what he considered his only so-so looks.

His friends *had* called him "Bucky Beaver" and "Mr. Peanut-head" in grade school.

But then he remembered how he had almost bolted out of the house later on that same night. He had called his old buddy, Tom, who came over, as always, with Joe. They just drove around the usual hang-out spots, comparing tits and asses. "Yup, I *am* straight like these guys, plain and simple," he'd thought.

Tom and Joe—why did he still spend so much time with them? Maybe he liked to be with them just because his Dad didn't like them. Whatever his reasons, Casey was going to choose his *own* friends and values. There's no way he would become a carbon-copy of his "all-knowing Dad."

Sunday, June 18, 1989

That was interesting, writing my diary like a novel. I think I'll try it again every now and then. It's fun, especially trying to think of titles to describe a particular episode in your life. Here's another try:

SALLY'S SURPRISING REVELATION

Every summer, for as long as he could remember, Casey always looked forward to coming to Granny McCoy's big, old white house at Cotuit, a sleepy little town that had somehow managed to stay virtually the same as the early years of Chuck's life, when he, too, left his hometown Boston for summers here with his family. Cotuit is on the southern coast of Cape Cod, protected by its own bay. It has just two grocery stores, a gas station, a post office, and a busy little harbor.

A week or so into their hiatus in Cotuit, Casey had awakened in a somewhat foul mood because of what he called his "transportation problem." He had saved up over a thousand dollars to buy a used motorcycle, but Chuck had vetoed his brainchild a couple of months ago because the insurance was too expensive and because of the safety factor. "Wait until you're eighteen," his father told him. "Then get one, if you still want one and can afford it." Rebelliously, Casey had spent most of the money on new audio equipment for his room as well as several splurges with Gloria and Mark. Now he was annoyed at himself that he hadn't enough money left to even buy an old clunker to cruise locally around the Cape. Since Chuck was in New York most of the time during the summer, he had to rely on borrowing Sally's when she didn't need it. He grudgingly admitted to himself that he encouraged Tom and Joe to come up to the Cape partially because of Joe's powerful old Chevy.

Casey's resentment towards his father flared up into outright hostility when, waking up with a smallish hangover, he discovered upon going downstairs for Sunday breakfast that Chuck had already left at 5 a.m. that morning for his office in New York to finish up work on some "Johnson case". Casey had forgotten which case that was, as he usually did. His lukewarm interest in his father's work was a response to his continual anger at Chuck's letting his work keep him away so much.

Still, Casey's crankiness wasn't enough to ruin his appetite for breakfast. It was a Sunday morning tradition at Granny McCoy's that they were all free to eat whenever they wanted, as long as they cleared up afterwards. Sally seemed annoyed at him as he eased into the dining nook next to Becky.

Becky mumbled, "Sal's after you, you creep, for not cleaning up the kitchen like you said you would after all those Cotuit guys left. The noise was bad enough without the mess." Becky really knew how to play on Casey's guilt.

"Shut up, you little cretin," he shot back. "I'm doing it right after breakfast so hold your horses for a while." Casey tried to give Sally a super-sincere look, "I promise I will, Sal. I'm sorry I forgot."

Sally said nothing, giving him one of her infrequent silent threats, an irritated glare which he translated as, "You'd better, or I'll be on your case until you do." But as usual, because he had credibility with her, his apology eventually worked. She finally smiled at him and asked if he wanted some coffee.

"Guatamalan?" he grinned eagerly.

"What else," she said filling up his jumbo mug.

Relieved, Casey could feel his irritability diminish as he sipped his daily caffeine "fix". Becky's needling he could do without, but he loved sitting with Sally in the huge, high-ceilinged, old-fashioned kitchen, with its magnificent huge cupboards and cabinets stacked full with all Granny McCoy's beautiful old dishes. Although Granny was now too old to cook much except for a couple of holiday dinners a year, the family still avoided using any of those ancient dishes for fear of breaking them.

He thought of his father again and reddened. "That bum. Why couldn't he have hung around, just for the morning at least?"

Becky raised her eyebrows. "C'mon, you turkey. You know how much he really wants to win that case so Susan Johnson can get back custody of her baby. How would *you* like to have your child taken away from you just because you're a lesbian?"

"Oh, you're always defending him, just because *you* get all his attention—'Daddy's little girl,' " Casey snarled out sarcastically.

Sally tried to intervene by offering some detachment. "You know, it's not uncommon for a girl to get most of her father's affection."

"I suppose so," grumbled Casey. "Anyway, all the McCoy men are work-junkies anyway."

"Well, it is true," Sally argued, "that Chuck's not so bad in comparison with your grandfather. You know that Chuck's father dropped dead of a heart attack at sixty-five, exactly a week after he retired. Now *he* was a true workaholic. Give your father credit. After all, he did refuse to work for his father's old-guard law firm. And instead he somehow persuaded its partners to set up a foundation to help financially strapped folks like adolescent runaways, mistreated racial minorities, and battered wives. He's given his life to helping them all. You could call that 'working within the system.' "

"I suppose so," Casey conceded, simultaneously shifting to Becky as his next target. He looked over at his fourteen-year-old sister, hardly able to believe the recent changes. About the only things that remained the same were Becky's sparkling blue eyes, freckles, and beaming smile. She had grown about six inches this past year and really filled out. Her long, brownish hair was now cut short (actually quite a bit shorter than Casey's, whose hair was now beginning its usual summer flirtation with his shoulders). Her choice hairstyle was a half-hearted attempt to fit in with sophisticated Westchester County teenage life, but, not wanting to be a carbon copy of everyone else, she had bleached only the ends blond. Becky had also confided that "Two years of all that gunky eye makeup was enough."

Casey had heard rumors that Becky had a new boyfriend, so being the obnoxious brother he was, he started asking obnoxious questions.

"Well, Becky, any big dates this weekend? You look ripe for a wild summer romance—or two."

"Actually, nitwit, I'm seeing Bobby Brayton this weekend, so if he's around the house, please refrain from being too silly. Bobby's not yet used to this weird family the way that Gloria is, you know."

"Don't worry, Becky," Sally said, "I know Casey will be on his best behavior—after all, he's gone through it all himself. He'll be rooting for you, won't you, Casey?"

"Yeah, yeah," Casey reluctantly agreed, trying to sound as if his answer promised little, if anything.

"You better, Casey," implored Becky, finally showing a weak spot. "Well, I'm going shopping. Got to find something decent to wear. See you later."

Casey raised his eyebrows, looking impressed, then turned to Sally, happy to be able to chat with her by himself. Sally was probably the most easygoing, good-natured mother, not to mention stepmother, that Casey had ever met. She had just finished her school year, having been assistant principal of the elementary school for five years. Although she'd done a fine job, she was quitting next year to return to teaching third-graders. She missed "the screams and whistles of the kids in the playground too much" and Casey loved her for that. But now she began to level with him.

"You annoy me sometimes, Casey—Chuck *has* improved. He's commuting less, even cleans up the house a bit now. He's a great father and you know it."

"I suppose so. Say, do you think it helped mellow him out to go to law school in the Bay Area in the late sixties? After all, that was the hard-core hippie era. I'm sure he worked hard there, but Mom has mentioned he began to let go a little when he started smoking grass then."

"Maybe. But he still holds a lot of things in." Sally got up rather abruptly and started clearing off the table. "I'm not complaining though, not really."

"Oh, Sal, leave that stuff. I said I'd do it. And go ahead and complain—you hardly ever do, you know. Dad does seem to be loosening up, though. Yesterday I saw something that looked promising. I accidentally stumbled into your bedroom again when it was occupied, only this time Pat was holding Dad—it was kind of neat. But I did wonder whether you'd approve or not, whether you'd be jealous."

"Oh, I suppose I could be, Casey. But I don't know that there's anything to be worried about." Sally sat down again and furrowed her brow. "Pat has his own happy life with Eddie and all their friends in Boston. You know he met Eddie seven years ago, just about the time your Dad and I started living together."

"Sal, it's just that I've always wondered about Pat and Dad. I know they were boyhood buddies before Pat moved away. And that they were sort of lovers in college. But what really happened? Was Dad scared of being gay?"

"No, I don't think so." Sally's brow furrowed again. "I don't know much about it—actually I don't want to know. It's *their* business after all and I totally trust Chuck. Maybe it'd help you to know that your mother, Diane, really put that relationship down. I think she was both scared by homosexuality and also somewhat threatened. She's admitted to me that she tried to blame Pat for all the troubles she and Chuck were having. Of course, she's changed a lot since then. Herb's been really good for her. I think she needed the time away from you kids—don't be hurt by that."

"C'mon, Sal. I've been really lucky—you, Chuck, Mom, Herb—Pat, too—you've all been great parents."

Sally said nothing in response. She may have been hoping for a change of subject. Casey, however, was not yet finished. "How about you, Sal. Have you ever had a crush on another woman?"

"Casey, my dear boy—or maybe I should say man—you're growing up quite rapidly, you know, much faster than our generation. Such tough questions."

"C'mon Sal, who is she?" Casey persisted.

"Well, it's no mad passion or anything but there *is* someone whom I've always had a little crush on. I knew her in college, Emilie's her name. She took off for France after graduation and has only returned a couple of times for short visits. She'll be here all next summer and has already reserved a couple of months at the Hodgkin's house. Don't get the wrong idea though. We're really just good friends. Well, time for tennis. Clean up your breakfast dishes, young man, or I'll be on the warpath!"

What a Mom! thought Casey later on. Actually he had two great Moms. He could hardly wait to go out west to Mill Valley to see Diane, his real Mom, next month. And he knew his buddy, Danny, would be cooking up all kinds of wild stuff to do.

As for his Dad, Casey couldn't throttle a surge of love for him. Chuck had sent him a card with a hundred dollars in it right when school ended, just after he had seen Casey's report card with all A's on it. Needless to say, the money was already spent, but Casey's appreciation remained. The note inside the card read:

To my wonderful son,

Congratulations. Here's something to help you stay fun-loving. Keep doing well and let the future take care of itself. Damn it—it would be unnatural if teenage kids knew exactly what their careers were going to be, so enjoy.

Love,
Dad

Casey knew he was free to major in anything he wanted to at college. He loved reading and writing up to a certain point, but he also thought of himself as the kid who was going to prove once and for all that lightning won't strike you down if you have fun, too.

Tuesday, June 20, 1989

I got a letter from Gloria today. She's stuck back in Hastings for a while yet, and I've been missing her a lot. Yes, I'm into my usual horny self too. Even when Gloria's around, I'm still never satisfied. I must have Congenital Horniness or maybe even Terminal Horniness. Anyway, forgetting about horniness for a moment, I want to state right here in a most unqualified fashion that Gloria is *wonderful*—how about this letter to help make a guy feel really good!

New York City, N.Y.
June 16, 1989

Dear Casey,

I LOVE YOU! I do miss you too, although life's frantic pace in the city helps keep me from dwelling on your absence. Also I've been doing museums and lots of movies too—the famous cultural life. Luckily it hasn't been very humid—not yet at least.

I'm writing to tell you I will be up on the Cape the weekend before the Fourth, so we'll have almost two weeks together before you take off for California. Mom was reluctant to lose my services, but I assured her I would keep working for her right up to the start of school. (Ugh, the thought of going back for one more year at HHS is almost unbearable—the sheer boredom factor.)

But not to worry. Mom'll let me keep taking occasional short breaks at the Cape. She knows I do need my time for fun. And she thinks you're good for me, too!

I hear "Hothead Tom" and Joe might be up there then too. Well, I guess I can handle that, although I still do sometimes wonder why you want to spend so much time around them—they don't exactly bring out your best side, but then that's only a woman's opinion. They must be very reassuring or something for you, I'm sure.

I'm about to go to the health club for a swim—if you don't get exercise in the city you start to go bananas. Oh, to be with you now, playing with your turquoise frisbee on the beach, seeing it float with the wind in the golden sunshine. Oh, to be up there in the loft with you, softly kissing your fantastic lips, smooching away, feeling a warm summer breeze wafting through the barn up into the loft and just looking into your bright, beautiful blue eyes. And then to hug you, snuggling up against you and drifting off together into space.

Just thinking of you cheers me up in this nuthouse. You've no rivals, not to worry, my dear Casey-cakes. New York men are so creepy—they all operate at about five times your rate of speed and, as a result, get maybe half as much done. Oh, instead to be melting into you, floating into ecstasy.

Back to real life. Mark told me he won't get up to the Cape until August. He knows it's usually a crummy month for weather, but he says that his courses in painting and photography down here won't be over until August 6th or so. I am really glad he's into them—he has got talent, lots of it and it's good for him to discover it. But the real reason I'm glad is that this last semester he was nearly getting completely turned off to education, not that high school can't be very boring, mind you. And since we're twins and I've been labeled the "smart one," it makes sense that he's tempted to do the polar opposite. Oh, I know you like that side of him, that high-on-life side, but it is becoming more of a macho phase now. He's into challenges and thrill-sports; I guess he needs those kinds of experiences, but I do hope he doesn't think he needs to prove himself or something.

It's been hard on him though, not having a father around. At least he and Mom have been really getting along well recently—they seem to be mellowing toward each other. I think Mark has pretty well acted out his hostility and rebellion. He's been such a brat the last couple of years that I've hardly had a chance to act out my own rebellious side.

That's all for now, Mr. Sweetie-Pie. I do love you very much and I will call you when I just can't stand it any longer.

Love,
Gloria

Ah, Gloria, a no bullshit relationship—or at least an attempt at one. Sometimes I wish we had more time for each other (i.e., she had more time for me.) Her Mom, Val, gave me some interesting advice over Memorial Day Weekend. "Casey, there's a much better chance you and Gloria will have a really first-rate relationship if she's allowed to have her own independent life, even though you two are already an established couple."

Val is usually right. I do get jealous and I sometimes feel it's my right to have Gloria all to myself, not for all time, but at least for a day or two, especially when we haven't seen much of each other. Another thing—I waited such a long time before Gloria and I started being sexual. I mean we were already friends as kids, and it was way more than a whole year between the time we first went out on a date and when we "made it" with each other. Just a few weeks ago she told me, "Casey, I was so surprised you wanted to go out with me because I'd always expected to fall in love with a stranger, someone I didn't know yet. And since we *had* been friends all our lives, the whole situation seemed to have the potential for getting too serious too fast—at least it did for me."

Not that I myself hadn't been looking around school for a strange, new, wonderful girlfriend—it's just that I never met anyone as great as Gloria. Being a lazy sort of guy, I said to myself, "Why fight it?"

But I've got to be careful with Gloria, not pressure her when she needs freedom. Practically speaking, I know from previous experience that my being the least bit pushy will get me nothing, zero, nada, from Gloria Gardner. Certainly I'm not ever going to be able to regress to your all-American, self-indulgent, male animal in this relationship.

My only problem is that there's a lot of raunchiness left in this guy. Or don't you have all these wild desires that I have, Gloria?

Saturday, June 24, 1989

Hastings-on-Hudson, N.Y.
June 22, 1989

Dear Casey,

I've lucked out. Both my classes have been cancelled on Friday, July 7, so I'm coming up for a long weekend. Prepare for some riotous living. Are you ready to run amok?

Two new additions: 1. Cancer-sticks. My only excuse is commuting every day to New York. 2. A moustache. Finally one that you can actually see.

My classes are great. Photography's a cinch—fun. I'm doing okay in my painting class, too. (Remember when we drew all those "explicit" pictures when we were twelve? And then showed them to your father?)

I miss swimming and the beach. But mostly I miss skiing. Hey, maybe I even miss you a little, you pervert. Keep in touch.

See ya,
Mark

P.S. I'm ready to trade sweatshirts again. How about if I get the purple one from you, you get the peach one from Gloria, and I pass the blue one on to Gloria?

I have to admit I was really missing Mark. I even thought about going down there to visit him. I'm glad he's coming here—much more fun.

I find myself still annoyed years later at Dad's comment after he looked at those "explicit" drawings—"Great, guys, the anatomy is perfect on both the boys and the girls. Looks to me, though, from these pictures, that you guys have left something out—maybe you don't believe that people of the same gender can have sex together."

Why does he still make stupid-ass comments like that? It's so ironic because he's the one who avoids sex with his own gender. Actually, I think Mark and I have both pretty much decided to join him in the ranks of those males who are exclusively straight. Life is so much easier that way.

Speaking of being straight, I'm happy to pass on the purple sweatshirt. It's really lavender and I sometimes feel like a sissy wearing it around Tom and Joe. Gloria, Mark and I have been sharing clothes for years. Those hooded sweatshirts are great for sailing on windy days, or for walking around on drizzly Cape nights.

Sunday, June 25, 1989

"Hothead Tom" and Joe have just left after an eventful weekend. (I sometimes feel guilty for having pinned that nickname on Tom. He used to have temper flare-ups in junior high, and once we had a fight in Mr. Alshat's class, so I've never let him forget it. He's basically an okay guy, though.) Anyway, it turns out that they can't come up later on, but Gloria will be here then, so that's just as well.

At least these guys are usually willing to have fun because they're not studying madly to prepare for college. When I ask them about their plans, they usually say they are going to stay around Hastings, maybe do some construction work, maybe go to Westchester Community College. They commute every day to a big Catholic school in White

Plains, mainly to please their parents, but they're only "C" students. The school's so strict I think they really need the release of going out drinking every now and then.

I met them a couple of years ago while playing basketball in a local village league. We all ended up on the same team and did fairly well, although none of us ever took the games that seriously. Tom's tall, about six foot three, really solid. He's pretty good-looking, too, and has dated a lot of different girls. It's hard to say whether he's blond or more of a red-head. He has very sensitive skin—it comes from being mostly Irish, I guess—he avoids hot days on the beach like the plague. Joe, on the other hand, is only about five foot ten, stocky, with lots of dark curly hair. Becky always refers to him as the "cute" one.

Sometimes after playing ball we go over to Joe's place on Hillside Avenue which is just across from the gym. Usually we like to horse around a bit in the locker room first—just the usual stuff—snapping jocks, fooling around with wet towels. Tom especially likes to parade around naked, pretending he's a stud in a porno movie. And then we'll go over to Joe's place and, sure enough, Mrs. Martino will whip out one of her homemade pizzas, throw it in the microwave and offer us soft drinks (except Joe always switches the Pepsis for beer the first moment she turns her back). Then, exhausted from our game, we settle in for some instant gratification.

It's their fathers who get to me. Both of them refused to go south when the copper mill closed. All they could find here were maintenance jobs, and so they are pretty bummed about America. They drink a lot, and sometimes get pretty out of hand.

Tom and Joe seem to spend almost all their waking hours together. It's convenient for them to commute to school together in Joe's Chevy and Tom's dad got them weekend jobs at the local A&P, but sometimes I think they bring out the worst in each other. Certainly, Sally and Gloria say they always bring out the worst in me and ask me why I spend so much time with them. Hell, they're my buddies. I like to hang out with them and have a beer or two.

Still, hanging around with them up here at the Cape sometimes isn't so hot. Until you're twenty-one in Massachusetts you don't have many choices—just drive-ins and chains along the trashiest parts of the Cape. Hyannis and Yarmouth used to be attractive towns, but now they're really bad...well, what really hurts is I end up hanging out at the very places I use as examples of the worst eyesores when I give Dad's colleagues the "royal tour" of the Cape. Anyway, the strip is dull here, but Tom and Joe like to ogle the women and watch an occasional brawl. That's where I part company with them—it's no thrill for me to watch someone get beat up.

Actually, when we were out last Saturday, I hoped we all might pick up some feminine companions for the evening, sort of, at least, but let's face it, what are the odds that three cruising guys can find suitable beauties to satisfy one and all—pure fantasy.

Anyway, here's the highlight of their visit recorded as another try at fiction:

A CLOSE CALL

If the first part of Saturday evening dinner at the local Bunny Burger was a bit boring for Casey, the second part proved exciting, too exciting. Around one in the morning, they left the youth of the Cape behind and jumped into Joe's monster Chevy. Luckily they haven't talked much about cars tonight, thought Casey; I just don't have much to say. Joe was pretty drunk and Casey was actually convinced as they sped along that they had gone off the road at least a dozen times. "The Wild Mouse was never like this," he said jokingly, hoping to get Joe to ease up on his reckless performance.

Then Tom, almost drunk, slipped into his rather gross, hostile personality. "Hey, you lunkheads, let's drive up to Provincetown and hassle some faggots."

Casey shrugged; he *could* have said, "Look, you meathead, I don't go for that prejudice stuff. My father's a lawyer whose career is defending all kinds of minority groups. You've even met our friends, Pat and Eddie. You can at least tolerate differences." What he actually said was, "C'mon, guys, let's go home—you know Dad likes me to be in by two unless I've told him I'll be later."

Heavy silence. Then Joe began going bananas at the wheel. Great Pond Road was full of twists and turns, and suddenly all that fast food and beer began to catch up with Casey. As the car went faster and faster around the turns, he began to feel sicker and sicker. Finally, he knew he'd have to throw up, but just as he leaned forward to try to get Joe to stop the car so he could get out, Joe took a curve too fast, forcing Casey's vomit to fly all over the car, propelled by centrifugal force. Scared by seeing his whole life pass before him, Casey begged to the powers-that-be in the universe, "Please, please, let us be able to at least crawl from the wreckage."

An instant later the car came to rest. It hung over the shoulder of the road, caught under some overhanging branches. The three guys determined with relief that there were no major injuries, although Casey was banged up a bit from ricocheting around the back seat. Tom glanced at Casey. "Yuck, why did you have to puke all over us." Just as Joe was about to see if the car would start, a cop happened upon the scene and pulled over.

"We're all too drunk to talk to this guy," thought Casey, suddenly feeling very clear-headed. He shuddered at the thought of his marijuana in the car, but luckily he had insisted they carry no open beer cans, a precaution Chuck had constantly drilled into him.

"You guys all right?" yelled the cop.

"Yeah, sure," said Joe.

"What the hell happened anyway? Say, is someone sick or something?"

Since Casey had been the one who puked, he suddenly felt responsible for explaining the situation. Besides Tom and Joe were so drunk that he figured they'd all immediately be thrown in jail if one of them tried to pronounce a word of more than one syllable.

"Officer, I got food poisoning tonight. These guys were trying to get me to the emergency room over in Hyannis. But I feel better now—I think vomiting enabled me to get rid of all the poisons or something."

"Better let me see the registration and your license," he demanded of Joe. "And both your ID's, you two."

We handed over the documents, not saying a word. Tom and Joe could have been wax dummies, they sat so still. The cop silently examined my license, then shined his flashlight right in my face. "Are you any relation to the McCoys in Cotuit, the family with all them lawyers? My brother's done a lot of repair work and landscaping for the old lady. He says she's a great ol' gal, feisty as hell sometimes, though."

"That's Granny McCoy!" replied Casey, not too enthusiastically, he hoped.

"Well, lookee here, Charles," said the officer to Casey with more than a touch of sarcasm in his voice. "Drunk driving is a very serious offense, especially by teenagers. Since your family's always been real nice to my brother, especially when he needed some legal help to get out of a mess a few years ago, I'm going to give your buddy here a break and just limit the penalty to a citation for reckless driving. And when you kindly repeat your phone number to me, Charles, I think I'll also give your Dad a call."

Casey thought of giving him a phony number, but quickly reconsidered when he realized how easy it would be for the cop to track down his father.

The cop copied down the number and told Joe to turn around and drive slowly back to Cotuit.

"I'll follow you for a while, just to make sure you're capable," he added with a slightly sinister tone.

Joe drove carefully back to the house. Casey asked Joe whether he had an extra shirt in the car, since his own T-shirt was covered with barf and he knew it'd be too suspicious to try to sneak into his house bare-chested at 2 a.m. "Nope," said Joe.

It finally didn't matter anyway, since Chuck flipped the porch light on and opened up the front door the exact moment they pulled up. He obviously knew already. On the way home, Casey had tried to convince himself how much worse it would have been if he had had to call Chuck from jail to bail them out on charges of drunk driving and possession of drugs.

So far he hadn't needed any help from Chuck's legal expertise, not even when he, Becky, Mark, and Gloria had all been temporarily detained in last fall's big anti-nuke demonstration. Though he knew Chuck would willingly help them out, Casey felt thankful that the first time was still in the future.

But when they reached the porch, something happened that Casey dreaded even more than a night in jail. Chuck gave him a half-loving, half-smug, quick eye-to-eye zap that wordlessly scored the great parental coup, "I told you so."

"Phew, someone stinks," said Chuck. "Get in here, you guys and thank your lucky stars you ran into one of the Riordan brothers. Otherwise you would have been in a mess of trouble. You know the local judges here don't much cotton to our way of thinking."

Once in the living room, Casey saw that Sally was also up. All he could do was try to look as ashamed as he could. Her look was piercing, but still forgiving. Chuck was somewhat angry at first, but after he got his sermon out of his system, he started seeing some humor in their dilemma.

Afterwards, while falling asleep, Casey decided he didn't want to risk life and limb any more just to hang out with Tom and Joe. But then he couldn't stop fantasizing about telling Mark what had happened. A part of him actually felt excited, exhilerated. Then too, he liked the fact that Tom and Joe had nothing to do with Hastings High or with Chuck and Sally's social world. They were *his* friends and he liked the sense of having a life of his own, away from his family.

Friday, June 30, 1989

This is the second summer at the Cape for my cat, Buzz, but the first one when he's old enough to get into fights. It's tough on him—male cats are so territorial. During the summer we yank him out of his regular territory, our yard in Hastings, and we bring him up here where he has to defend new turf. It's such a contrast when he's with people, because then he's all sweet and gentle, except for an occasional tooth 'n claw attack when you stick your hand in his tummy and he's in a feisty mood.

Buzz is all-white, but his nose, paws, and ears are pink, like a bunny-rabbit's. Almost every night he snuggles in my bed with me. First thing I always wipe away any boogers from underneath his eyes since they show up so clearly on a white cat. Sometimes we both burrow under the blankets together, then he rolls over against me, gives me kisses, and plays at digging his claws into me. It's all really a turn-on, except for the claws.

But then he gets up before dawn, and the trouble begins. In his punk-o alley-cat scene, he often gets hurt by more hard-hearted, veteran fighters. I can hardly stand it when he gets hurt. I feel too much for him; we're so close. I should detach myself a little. Like now there's a big swelling over his right eye. He hates to be nursed by anyone, especially a vet, but it does look like we're going to have to grab him out of the house, stuff him in the car, and ignominiously deliver him to the vet.

Yesterday he caught a bird. I pried it free, and it flew away. I guess it was okay. I was so relieved. But I have the same feelings towards the birds he catches as towards him when he's hurt. Life in the food chain—I guess there's a lot of hunting and preying in nature, in all of us. However, I'd just as soon we humans were all vegetarians, and that I could get through life without having to see anybody or anything in pain. It'd be easier to feed everybody too. Yesterday I got bummed out all morning when I saw pictures in the *Times* of all those starving kids in Asia.

One of Danny's good lines from California came to me and picked me up a bit. His dentist in San Francisco supplies him a pleasure-palace of laughing gas, rock music, and euphoric drugs. "Dr. Aldente and I have worked out a good relationship," Danny says with his flashing eyes. "He knows I can't stand pain."

I can't stand pain either—for me or anyone else.

Sunday, July 2, 1989

Val's here and Gloria's coming in a couple of days. I'm really enjoying Val's company. She's looking so good—short dark hair, good tan, hardly any make-up—you'd guess she's just thirty. She moves so energetically, but she's calm too, especially since she started doing some meditating.

Luckily for Becky and me, Val was around when Mom freaked out. Val's an incredibly strong person. Her husband had just plain disappeared a year earlier, 1977. However, because they had bought their house before inflation hit, she had fairly low payments on the mortgage, and she was able to support herself and the kids by commuting to New York to a good-paying job on Wall Street. She's still with this firm owned by women that specializes in helping other women decide how to invest their money. While working there, she became philosophical about her husband's ditching her and her kids (the twins were four when he split.) Instead of resenting him, she just shrugged her shoulders and said, "It was just as well. We would have destroyed each other." Apparently he drank a lot and sometimes beat her.

At first she was guilty about being a single parent and having to send the kids to day care centers, so she let Gloria and Mark run all over her. Then some of the women she worked with got her to join a group for single mothers, and she caught on to how she was being manipulated, letting Gloria and Mark, who were both really wild then, take advantage of her. Soon her bosses valued her work so much that they made her a partner and she was able to do some of her work at home in Hastings. Then she and Sally started babysitting for each other's kids when we weren't at school.

Val's house is about six doors down from us in Hastings. Our neighborhood isn't anything special, not like the posh ones up on the hills in Riverview Manor or Hudson Heights, but it still has lots of nice old houses with lush yards and big beautiful trees. (I love green, jungle-type vegetation. That's one thing I don't like about California—the dry, brown hills in the summer.) We have an old, slightly run-down, sprawling place that Chuck and my Mom, Diane, bought at a bargain price in anticipation of their having a large family. Val's place is much smaller, just perfect for the three of them since each of them has a little bedroom.

Anyway, when Mom and Dad started fighting all the time and finally broke up in 1978, Val showed Dad how he was aggravating the situation by being so uncommunicative with Diane. When Mom really flipped out, it was Val who encouraged Mom to move back to the Bay Area for a "clean slate". Mom had loved it out there while Dad was going to law school at the University of California. Of course, though, Mom felt very guilty about leaving Becky and me with Chuck, but Val promised her that she'd help Chuck out.

It sure hasn't been easy for either family. Sometimes poor Chuck would become so exasperated with us kids that *he'd* look like he might break down. But when we got a little older, he met Sally. Then everything changed.

Val, herself, had some very tough years trying to handle Gloria. There was a period there, about 1984-1986, when Gloria became a teenager, during which she and Val fought all the time about make-up, about staying out late, even alcohol and drugs. Luckily, Gloria somehow got through most of what she calls her adolescent rebellion by the time she turned fourteen. So Val and she became friends. It was then that Gloria started thinking seriously about a career, about becoming a doctor, maybe even a surgeon who made sure that the particular problems women had weren't misdiagnosed by male surgeons who she suspected might be a little too eager to operate a lot of the time.

As you can see, our two families have remained really close over the years. Val gets out to visit Diane in Mill Valley at least twice a year and usually comes up here to the Cape a few times each summer—I think of the blue upstairs bedroom as hers. And the little, sunny pink bedroom is Gloria's. Of course, since I've been ten, I've had my own place back behind the house in the barn, up in the loft actually. It even has its own furniture—old wicker chairs and weird little bureaus that must be a least a hundred years old. Gloria still uses that little pink bedroom to have her own space, but that makes her visits to the loft even nicer.

Wednesday, July 5, 1989

Here we go again! The novelist in me loved writing this one.

HAPPY DAYS ARE HERE AGAIN!

Casey could tell instantly that all was not right with Gloria the moment he met her at the bus station in Falmouth, Friday night of the big holiday weekend. He placed her bags in the trunk, and they had started the drive back to Cotuit through the familiar scrub oaks and pines. He immediately began deluging her with all the fun things they were going to do to that weekend. But Gloria was wiped out from a month of commuting to New York City to her summer job, and the bus ride probably hadn't improved her spirits, either. Immediately, in Casey's view of things, she "got on his case."

"Pleez, Casey, do give me at least a moment to catch my breath. You know sometimes I do have some serious trouble dealing with your intensity. I'm always supposed to be ON. You aren't like this with everyone else, I bet."

"But, Gloria, isn't it expected that a guy be really enthusiastic about having fun with a super-wonderful girlfriend like you? Forgive me for trying to get as much as I can of this rare visit from you."

"Watch the sarcasm, please," Gloria warned, but her face started to relax, and she smiled. "Sometimes I think it would be better if you didn't think of us—and our time together—as so special. You know I love you. But I've just got out of the city. I need to unwind before I can really enjoy you or the Cape."

"Okay, I see your point," said Casey, only slightly crestfallen.

"And another thing," Gloria wasn't finished with him yet, "Try to remember that you don't actually own me. Even though the media does program us otherwise, you can't always assume I want to be with you more than my girlfriends at any given time."

She was so irritable that Casey should have just sat and listened. Instead he tried to be humorous. "Okay. Okay. It's not that important if you're not around. I'll just go up to the loft, all aching and lonely. I can always beat off to relieve my tension."

As soon as these words came out, he regretted them. She really let him have it.

"Don't be an asshole, Casey. You and your constantly aching-to-be-satisfied sexuality. I love you, but I sometimes think our love-making is based primarily on *your* needs."

Casey just kept on driving as if everything was still okay, but inside he felt fear down in the pit of his stomach.

"What I really mean," she resumed after a long pause, "What I really need is more experiences with other people, so I can explore myself more."

"Anything you want," Casey replied, relieved that her tone had lost its hostile edge.

"It makes me guilty to bring this up—it's something a woman's not supposed to do. But I bet you want to see other people too. I'm only suggesting that we need to communicate more about this stuff as situations come up—I'm hardly saying we should go out and become wildly promiscuous with the rest of the human race. Well, what do you think?"

Casey just kept driving for a few minutes. He had to admit to himself that she could be justified, that he just might think of her too often as "my girl." Maybe his initial feeling of insecurity was premature. After all, she was only trying to improve their relationship.

"So you still really love me?" Casey pouted, acting ourageously like a hurt child seeking sympathy.

"You know I do. C'mon, forgive me for being so crabby. I should have waited to get the city out of my system before bringing this stuff up. Face facts, Casey. You know you'll benefit just as much, maybe even more, if we can figure this stuff out. You love freedom just as much as I do. For instance, your relationship with Mark. It's pretty much okay with me, but I don't completely believe you when you keep saying that it's a thing of the past, and that it was only 'kid stuff.' "

Yuck. Casey had not wanted this subject brought up, so he tried to finesse his way out by agreeing with her general premise. "Okay, okay. You're right. We both need to explore some more with other people. And we will—but that's in the future. So let's return to the present. Did you know Becky's not going to be around this weekend?"

"She's up in Cambridge studying her clarinet, isn't she?" Gloria apparently was willing to go along with Casey's highly obvious ploy to change the subject.

"It's intimidating, you know," he observed, "what with your wanting to be a surgeon and her a symphony conductor and me—I don't know what the hell I'm doing."

Gloria laughed in a way that showed Casey she admired him the courage of his convictions. "Yes, but, to have any chance at all, she has to start young. I, for one, am looking forward to seeing her play at the Music School's Summer Festival in a couple of weeks. And she's actually going to get a chance to conduct a piece before the end of the summer session."

"We've sure become good friends in the last year," Gloria continued, "since she too escaped from the mascara and green eye-shadow phase. Hey, she told me that you were teasing her a lot about her date with Bobby Brayton."

"Gloria!" Casey tried to register total shock. "I was on my best behavior and she even thanked me afterwards. Don't forget how much she teased *us* when we started going out, how she'd even follow us and spy on us whenever she could."

And so, with the ice broken, the two lovers fell into the usual rhythms of the Fourth of July weekend at the Cape: the family dinner on Friday, sailing the skiffs on Saturday morning, the slightly boring cocktail party at the Emersons on Saturday night, the big fireworks display later that night, the picnic on Sunday afternoon and finally, camping together on Waponsic Island Sunday night.

As Casey piloted the skiff towards the island, he thought about how great it was having Gloria around. It wasn't just that she was sexually attractive; it was her whole person that he found so exciting. Her bright, blue eyes and long lashes, her sensual lips, her smooth but solid shoulders—Gloria had swum out to this island many times. She was a great swimmer and hiker—it was just as if you were with Mark when you were out in the woods with her. But then she could look super-luscious in a dress for a job interview or formal dance. Yum, that soft, velvety skin, those long, bare arms. There was something about her being both a tomboy and a stunning woman that really turned Casey on. But, most of all, it was that doesn't-give-a-damn-what-anyone-thinks side of her that drove him wild with desire. That vital spark and that almost careless way about her physical presence. What self-confidence! Casey had never been more madly in love with her than now.

They soon reached their chosen campsite, Casey's favorite sand dune. Their little fire made up for the drop in the air temperature after a beautiful sunset and its afterglow. They were lying around naked on top of their sleeping bags, with their dinner just about digested. Just as they started in with some soft kisses, they heard noises in the distance from a bunch of younger guys who had apparently convinced their folks that they could spend the night on the island. They didn't notice the lovers, but at first Casey thought they would ruin the whole romantic atmosphere. The kids started rough-housing, teasing each other, drinking beer, even making dirty jokes. Gloria just listened with a silly, contented smile on her face. Then one of guys suggested smoking a joint of super-zonko California weed. Soon they all became very quiet and seemed vibed into the island's beauty, with the moon on the water (almost a full moon, definitely a crazy, horny one) and the stars. They started playing tapes they had brought with them—old stuff like Van Morrison, Brian Eno, the Talking Heads, the Dead, and even the

Beatles. Gloria and Casey just purred and made love.

One thing's for sure. He really appreciated Gloria after not seeing her for a while. Another thing was for sure; Gloria's a woman who wouldn't let him take her for granted—fat chance that he would anyway.

Monday, July 10, 1989

Mark's been here for the weekend and we've had *lots* of fun. Sometimes it's hard to believe that he and Gloria are actually brother and sister, much less twins; they seem so different in some ways. Mark has so much good energy, but I guess he sometimes forces it, as if he needs to be high all the time and to be constantly on the move—even when he sits around, he's always cracking his bones, bouncing his knees up and down, or tilting back precariously on his chair.

But he's such a gas—we always have a good time together. Take yesterday. We had decided to spend the whole day at the tip of the Cape, at Pervert-town, as I like to call it when I want to get Dad to give me a "don't be prejudiced" look. Ha, Dad was funny when I told him we wanted to go there. He was more than willing to let me go just so I could see different kinds of life-styles for myself. He even gave us spending money and called it a "field trip." Meanwhile, Gloria said she was already committed to an evening with a girlfriend, and, with that mischievous sparkle in her crystal-clear eyes, told me mock-sternly, spoofing her own typical propaganda, "You know I'd never betray one of my sisters in order to spend time with a man."

Actually, I was kind of glad when Gloria said she wasn't coming. I felt like being alone with Mark—we have this sense of being like kids exploring together. We're curious about everything and we don't care how people react to us.

We can turn any situation around; you just can't stop us from having fun together.

And, boy, did we have fun yesterday, even though I had some trouble with the vibes there. It's not that we got uptight or anything. I'm always pretty comfortable when gays visit our family, for instance.

Anyway, while driving out there, Mark and I got to exchanging stories about how we had been hassled by weird men while hitch hiking. "Last summer," said Mark, "I was hitching to Buzzard's Bay to go see my aunt on the Vineyard. This guy in his forties in a BMW picks me up, and after no more than two minutes and zero conversation suddenly asks me if I want a blow job. I tell him '*no thanks*' very plainly and start trying to figure out how to get out of the car fast. Well, he doesn't seem violent or anything, so I just sit there, without saying a word, for another fifteen minutes, until we get to Buzzard's Bay. Then, after getting out at the ferry landing, I pick up a few small stones and skid them across the top of his car as he drives off, just to let him know how I felt."

"Maybe that was good for him," I answered. "I mean he could get killed if he propositioned the wrong person. I had an experience like that too, last summer when I was hitchhiking out in California."

"What happened?" asked Mark, both curious and slightly disgusted.

"Well, I was hitching around Sacramento, all grubby from camping for a few days in the Sierra. I had just about given up any hope of getting back to Mill Valley that night, but I didn't know where to stay. I was marooned in uptight suburbia, hadn't had a ride for a couple of hours. Finally this guy comes along, sort of like the one you mentioned, in his forties, short, thinning hair, a little paunchy. Of course I gladly accepted the ride. After a few minutes he asks me if I want to clean up at his place and have a bite to eat. Well, the offer sounded good to my stomach, so I accepted.

"He had this big, ranchstyle house, with pictures of his wife and kids all over the place. First he shows me where the bathroom is and hands me a towel. Then he hangs around and kind of sneaks glances at me while I'm in the shower. I'm not really scared because I see the pictures of the family and everything and I'm also curious as to what his trip is. After I get dressed, he asks me if I want to see a sex movie. So I get a sandwich and sit down in front of this big screen in his incredibly equipped video room and watch this terrible movie, all straight couples making love. Before the movie's over I can feel his hand on my shoulder, and, just as the movie ends, he asks me if I want a blow job. I tell him no. So then he asks if he can just touch my penis. I tell him that I'm not into *any* sex with men.

"So then after these awkward silences, he becomes very friendly again and asks me if I want to spend the night. You won't believe this, Mark, but I actually felt a little fear about being raped or something. Anyway, I know I don't want to stay, so I emphatically insist that I have to get back on the road. Well, then he becomes really nice and offers to drive me to the bus terminal. He calls up the bus company and finds out that I can catch a bus to San Francisco in half an hour. So that's what I did. Another late bus, this one to Mill Valley, so I still make it home and everything. Hell, I think the guy was just plain lonely—I mean he was mixed-up, but pretty harmless."

"Probably," said Mark, "but I wish those kind didn't act so hard-up for sex with younger guys. That experience kind of ruined it for me any time a man touches me now."

"I know what you mean. Well, let's just play it cool today and stick to ourselves."

So after driving out there, we ended up at the nude beach and got as far away from the crowd as we could, up on a dune so we could look down on the spectacle below. We took off our clothes, of course. (Mark and I have been going to these kind of beaches since we were fourteen; that's the age I got over being uptight about it. Ha, when we used to go to nude beaches in California with Mom and Herb, all the parents would be naked, and all us embarrassed kids kept covered up.) We did see a lot of guys wandering around, but we figured they weren't gay because most of them had girlfriends whom they were steering around. Those types almost never take their clothes off, but they're still curious, I guess.

Anyway Mark and I pretty much stuck to our decision not to get involved with anyone we met on the beach. Actually, if we met some really nice people, we might have been open to getting to know them—we were just on our guard.

Of course, lying there in the sand, you focus on bodies. I felt pretty good about mine—I'm not as wiry as Mark who is very thin, yet amazingly strong for his weight. Mark is super-blond, with wild, tangly, long, bleached chaotic hair, with those intense, laughing blue eyes. His body almost buzzes with energy when he's near you. He seems to generate warmth as he talks a mile a minute and establishes body contact in a spontaneous way, as if he *has* to share his good feelings with you. After a couple of beers he lounges around in don't-give-a-damn positions on the beach. It's so easy to relax and let go with him around.

Even with his moustache, which is as blonde as his hair, he still looks just about the same. I guess he's trying to look more like a man now, not a kid.

Well, just as we were getting into a beach melt-down, somewhere between bliss and blotto-consciousness, the parade of gays starts. Now I think it's fine that everyone walks around cruising each other at these beaches. I mean, in a way, that's what the beach scene is for. It's the *heavy* looks and weird game-playing I don't dig. But no one bothered us. I kept the potentially obnoxious ones away with my cold, hard stare—and the nice ones would just drop by for a minute or two, but then move on when we gave real short answers to all their questions.

Anyway there were some small waves in the afternoon. We had some good swimming and got a lot of sun. (I'm the darkest I've ever been right now, still with something of a tan line.) Later we hung out in P-Town some more and wandered around all these neat, winding streets. We almost hooked up with a couple of really attractive college women. You could tell they were tempted, but felt reluctant to go out with guys who were so young. We walked by a lot of gay bars and hang-outs. Some places were wild with energy. Other places felt a little creepy. It was all okay, though.

Saturday, July 15, 1989

New York City, N.Y.
July 13, 1989

Dear Casey,

How are you doing? I bet you're having a great summer out there. The city hasn't been all that humid yet, but we all know it's coming. It sure helps me to feel better knowing I'll be cooling off up there on the Cape with you in a while, away from all these exhaust fumes.

I wanted to tell you about something. I'm planning to attend a seminar for high school seniors on the psychological theories of Carl Jung—it's at Columbia on Saturday mornings in November and December. Maybe you could take it too; it's free if your grades are good enough and I already know you've mastered the art of how to get A's and still have a lot of fun.

The usual kvetch about my parents. I just don't think they will ever know me. At least they pretty much leave me alone most of the time.

Anyway, Casey, I will not hide from you the fact that I'm really looking forward not only to seeing you, but also Chuck and Sally and the whole gang. I've seen Chuck for lunch a couple of times this summer here in the city. You're so lucky to have him for a Dad. Thanks for sharing your world with me.

Your friend,
Rob

It was good to hear from Rob. I really like him, though I suspect that he's gay. Actually he hasn't tried at all to pretend he's heterosexual; he just hasn't said anything. Most people would never guess he's gay. He's big, 6′ 2″, brown eyes, brown hair, still growing, very strong, and acts pretty much just like any other guy. I'm a little scared of his not being scared of me. With my straight male friends, I always know they'll hold back. I mean I'm the least macho, the most guy-liking of all the guys I know. With Rob, I guess I'm afraid because I sense I could have a deeper friendship with him than with any other guy I know. It's *not* because I'm afraid I might be gay. A little AC-DC type action might even be okay for a while. C'mon Casey, you don't need to go all over that one again. It's just that I'm a little confused and need more time to think things out.

I met Rob almost two years ago, in the fall of our sophomore years, at Columbia University's annual conference for the staff members of high school newspapers. Gloria and I were there as the young hot-shots from the Hastings *Buzzer* along with the junior and senior big wigs. Working on the paper together helped us get to really know each other before we dated. (No big surprise—she's Editor next year.) Anyway, she had met Rob at a symposium on how to write editorials and invited him to have lunch with us. We all got along so well I invited him out to dinner Friday night, right after the conference ended, with Chuck, who had said he'd treat Gloria and me.

Chuck and Rob really hit it off that evening. When Gloria asked Chuck about his defending a gay man who was fired by his company when it became known that he was a homosexual, Rob became totally attentive and soon joined our conversation about whether or not the country was becoming more politically repressed. At the end of the evening Chuck invited Rob to visit him at his office. Rob took him up on the offer and Chuck soon became a kind of surrogate father for him. Sometimes I resent Chuck for being available for Rob because Chuck always claimed he never had time to play ball or go fishing with me when I was younger. Usually, though, I admire Chuck for being there to help others.

I'm sure Rob's talked to Chuck about his being gay. I know he could never talk to his own parents about it. Dad's invited him to our place for some weekends and he spent a lot of time at the Cape with us last summer. Around early August or so he started being openly physical with me, stuff like putting his arm around my shoulder when we went out for walks at night. No one saw us or anything, but I acted like I was more uncomfortable than I actually was because I was afraid he'd start acting that way in front of some of the crowd I hang around with in Cotuit. He got my message though, and it's no problem now. I can pretty much relax with him lately and look forward to his visits.

Wednesday, July 19, 1989, Mill Valley, CA.

Here I go again, being my bi-coastal self, out at Mom's house in Mill Valley for my annual summer visit. Mom and

Herb bought it two years ago. It's mostly on one floor, with a small lower level that Danny uses. It's got some redwoods planted around the yard, but there's still plenty of sun in both the front and the back. And the back yard is very private so we can use the new hot tub they got last winter any time we want. It's a big house, with weathered wood shingles on the outside, cedar, I think. There's a huge living-room complex with a massive fireplace, a couple of couches and lots of open space. The kitchen is very modern, big, and comfortable, with plenty of room for the breakfast table in front of a big window which lets the morning sun stream in.

I've been noticing the differences in summer between the coasts. Back home, it's getting humid. The marigolds are all getting bigger, and you can smell honeysuckle on warm days. Here the humidity is much lower, the same with the average temperature, except during heat-waves. It's almost always sunny in the afternoons, but sometimes there's morning fog. (Since I'm talking about Mill Valley, which isn't quite on the coast, I should mention the fog can stay all day on the coast, just like the Cape.) Outside of the well-watered suburban gardens, everything's dry here, except if you go hiking in a redwood glade, which feels moist and refreshing even on a sweltering day. I like the feel of redwood bark and the way the baby eucalyptus leaves are so different from those on the grown-up trees. I love to see huge fields of artichokes when there are *thousands* of artichokes ready for picking. I *love* artichokes.

I also love to go jogging up the fire roads of Mt. Tamalpais on a hot day and come racing home, all downhill, hot and sweaty. Then I throw off all my clothes and collapse on Danny's waterbed and just let every tension in my body drain into the water. And then a few minutes later into the hot tub.

Ah, the good life in California. Take this morning.

"Casey, Becky, have some more breakfast. There's lots more fruit—cherries? Strawberries? Apricots? How about more hot cakes—yogurt—more tea? C'mon. You're both going to have busy days today."

"Thanks Mom, I'm stuffed," said Becky.

"Don't worry, Mom, just leave the fruit out and I'll take care of it before the end of the day. It was a great breakfast—and so was dinner last night too. You really treat us well when we're out here," Casey added.

"Well, darlings, you know I'm still trying to lure you both out here to spend more time with Herb and me."

"Be careful, Mom. You know I'm pretty sure about going to college in California. I opened up a checking account out here to prove my residence so we can take advantage of in-state tuition rates. You know I do appreciate both your and Dad's willingness to subsidize my education, but I'm going to do some of it by myself. That way I won't feel so guilty if I drop out for a while and travel. I want my education on my own time schedule."

"It's okay with me, Casey. Ever since my 'breakdown', I've respected the judgment of both you and Becky. You kids proved your mettle during those hard times—you put up with a lot of crap from me. Thank God for Anne. She was exactly the kind of therapist I needed to help me finally start my own life. Still, those were tough years out here. I was a bundle of nerves until just before I met her."

"Mill Valley is so beautiful it makes me want to move out here right now. Those Eastern winters—yuck," Becky grimaced. "I've been noticing in the newspapers that there's a lot going on musically, too."

"I'm betting that both you kids will eventually end up out here. I'm looking forward to the time—it's practically here now—when you'll both be more like friends than kids."

"Hey, Mom, you already are my friend, that is, now that you don't become so hysterical all the time," Becky teased. "Wow, you got your career together too, plus a good relationship with Herb. You've worked really hard at becoming happy."

"It was all worth it. I love working with families, and Herb works one-to-one with his clients—so we get a chance to compare techniques, results, whatever. Right, Herb?"

"You bet," answered Herb who had just sat down to join the group. "We're the local champs at that fine California sport you play on your keister—psycho-babble!"

"Seriously, Herb, do you apply your therapy stuff to your relationship with Mom?" Casey's curiosity was piqued by the relative absence of such defined techniques in the relationship between Chuck and Sally.

"With a grain of salt—sure, at least a little. Sometimes it's a bit messy, with all our 'processing' and 'discharging,' eh Diane? But we hang in there pretty well."

"It's nothing like the messiness I went through during those tough years. Sometimes it's painful working through problems with Herb, but it's always constructive."

"Well, at least we act out our weird stuff. Then, with that junk ventilated, there's a chance of approaching some sort of sanity."

And so it went. I've really come to enjoy Herb as a kind of uncle in the last few years. He still has that wry, ironic style of talking, but I swear he looks much younger than he did five years ago. He was already pretty gray then. I think he has a bit more white in his beard, but his face seems so much younger because he's so relaxed. He no longer has to be the big-deal therapist making speeches about psychological stuff and taking himself so seriously. His favorite line this trip is, "I like you, but I don't want to have sexual intercourse with you."

As for Mom, what a change in the last few years too! She's lost a lot of weight from a few years ago and is so tan she hardly uses make-up. I love those huge, golden earrings she likes to wear and her hair looks great a little shorter. She wants me to go to her church tomorrow, but no way.

(She's always saying, "Let go and let God.") That Unity stuff seems fine for her, but tomorrow's supposed to be warm and sunny at the ocean, and Danny and I are planning a big day of sun, beer, and who knows what?

Tuesday, July 25, 1989

A "HARD" DAY AT THE BEACH

Sunday morning dawned bright and clear. Danny and Casey eagerly put their morning chores behind them so they could get an early start for the beach. Driving the scenic, twisting, redwood-explosion of Panoramic Drive as it descended Mt. Tamalpais, Casey's heart pounded just a bit as they looked down to see the glassy ocean below. Yes—no fog or wind, at least not yet. They had a couple of wetsuits with them, and Danny told Casey that, with the high tide now beginning to ebb, there was a good chance of decent waves, since the swell often picked up in the afternoon as the tide pulled back.

Eager as he was for waves, Casey was even more eager for something else—women. Danny and he definitely understood each other in this particular area of life. Danny, in fact, had just broken up with his girlfriend at the beginning of the summer. He told Casey, confidentially, that it had been a slow, horny summer so far, but the couple of sexual experiences he did describe made Casey ready for just about anything. He loved feeling this tingling sense of adventure.

After descending the long, serpentine path to the beach, they agreed on a spot in a sheltered nook and quickly took off all their clothes. Danny was a typically good-looking California blond, with blue eyes, perfectly even teeth (unlike Casey), and both a face and a body Casey couldn't help envying somewhat. He reminded Casey of Mark a little, although Danny was somewhat less hyper, somewhat less "magical" too, although definitely better looking, at least the way most people would see it. Danny wasn't as thin as Mark either—who could be? He was strong, solid, although he probably weighed only about 160 pounds at maybe six feet tall.

As he undressed, Casey couldn't suppress a moment of self-doubt about his own body, his looks, his cock, his physical strength as compared to Danny's. Then he caught himself and remembered he had gone over this list many times over the years. Once again, he decided he was okay. He was taller by about an inch, a bit thinner, with dirty blond hair that was just now getting bleached out by the sun. Danny was as blond as Mark, very tan, but with shorter, neater, and straighter hair than Mark's wild, chaotic, frizzy mess. Ha, thought Casey, no mother could possibly like Mark's mop, although he guessed Val came pretty close to accepting it.

A love of freedom—in fact, an insistence on freedom. That was the quality Danny shared with Mark.

After spreading out their towels, Casey immediately responded to the slight salt tang in the air (he thought the Atlantic was saltier), and the sweet smell of someone's coconut oil. A flock of about twenty brown pelicans drifted south on the slight sea breeze. Then Casey saw Danny smile. He turned around as Danny had done to check out the scene behind them. Lo and behold!—three outrageously beautiful creatures, all about sixteen or seventeen. They had apparently never been to a nude beach before, since they had tan lines with a vengeance, the outline of their very brief bikinis being very evident—and sexy. The fact that these sweet things were also having a new experience further excited Casey. What lay ahead on this beautiful day?

Danny and he had, of course, brought a couple of sixpacks, so after sunning themselves for ten minutes or so, Danny, without even asking Casey, looked back and started a conversation with the young ladies, offering them a beer and some of his homegrown weed. Right then, alas, Casey knew it was all over between him and these sweet young things, for all three of them declined *both* grass and booze. And yet Danny continued to chat away with them. They were from a fairly uptight inland town and had crossed over the rocks from the nearby state beach out of curiosity. Oh, and all three were so appealing—perfect bodies, beautiful breasts; you could see they sort of wanted to act naughty at the beach. Didn't Casey know better than to hope for any future action with any of them? To people with such conventional value systems, Danny and he must seem too wild, too strange.

After some more pleasant chatter, with Casey joining in, the boys turned around to look at the ocean so that their backs now faced the girls. It was time to get ripped before going in the cold water. Immediately after a quick beer and a few puffs on a joint, Danny and Casey donned their wet suits and dove into the 60-degree water, barely noticing the cold. And there were waves! The afternoon swell had come up simultaneously with a moderate breeze. How big? Three or four feet, maybe. But, who cared about measuring them—they were well-shaped and had a lot of punch, great rides with a devastating wipe-out every now and then. Danny and he stayed in nearly an hour, until they were almost too exhausted to wade up onto the shore.

When they returned to their spot, the girls were all lying flat on their backs as if asleep. Danny and he had another beer. Casey was feeling happy and high, anticipating the glorious pleasure of letting the sun blast him back to warmth. Ah now, now was the perfect moment for the melt-down. But just as Casey was closing his eyes, he happened to notice Danny's penis; Danny was also flat on his back, seemingly asleep, as if he were no longer taking responsibility for what his cock was doing!

What was it doing? It was growing bigger at an alarmingly fast rate. A surge of sexual energy shuddered through Casey as he realized what his demented California relative was up to. He definitely was a bit taken aback at Danny's unconcern in relation to the trio of spectators just behind him. Luckily, he thought, it wasn't that obvious to the rest of the beach since, lying on his back, Danny's penis only sprang out from his body at about a 45-degree angle. Yet that was plenty of rise to make it obvious to the girls that Danny now had a definite erection. In fact their view, a few feet away, on a slightly higher incline, had to be the best seat in the house.

So Danny had decided to simply show off his desire for them. Or maybe it was his sheer love affair with the sun, since the lethal combo of beer, dope, and sun always caused one's system to really pump out the testosterone. The girls now had a free choice. They could look or not as they pleased.

Hmm. Why not, thought Casey. He wasn't too stubborn to be a copycat, given a good enough reason.

Just then, to make his notorious deed even more obvious, Danny turned his body so that he was resting on one elbow in the sand, facing directly towards the girls. Casey did the same so that his feet almost touched Danny's. He closed his eyes quickly, for he could already feel his own cock stiffening. So here they were! He felt naughty, but he also marveled at Danny's—and his own—nerve. Somehow the girls had communicated that they'd go along with the outrageous display.

After a few minutes, Casey's desire became less intense, less sexual. Now it all seemed not so sexual, but just what anyone would feel on a happy day, lying in the sun, just letting go.

A half hour passed—no one moved. He was dozing on and off. Clearly, the girls weren't running off freaked out or anything. Every now and then he and Danny would get up for a beer. Once, Danny got up to piss in a nearby cave. After a half-minute or so, Casey realized he had the same need. As he went for the cave, Danny came out, his cock standing just about straight up. With both of them obviously on their way to the land of Blotto Consciousness, Casey and Danny slipped casually into basketball-player-style behavior, slapping each other's hands with a high-five. Although it was a weird scene, for one brief moment Casey had the urge to throw his arms around Danny's shoulders and hug him just for being so outrageous.

The moment passed. Soon the boys re-assumed their initial positions on their backs, both aroused once again. This time it felt as if a sensible routine had already been established. Fifteen more minutes passed. Then one of the trio looked at her watch and indicated to the others that they must leave right away. The boys turned over on their stomachs and the girls got up to go, not neglecting to wave good-bye to the guys who were now in a blissful half-stupor.

* * *

I'll just summarize the rest of Sunday. A few of Danny's high school friends showed up later in the afternoon. After we had another couple of swims, we all left the beach together and arrived back in Mill Valley about five. Herb and Diane were out. Danny and I were still cold from swimming so much, and the hot tub soon beckoned. We stripped down, jumped in and were joined by Danny's friends a few minutes later. Keeping up his reputation for the bizarre, Danny started playing footsy in the hot tub, comically feeling around a bit. Everyone laughed, for they knew him well and enjoyed his antics without taking him seriously. Then, we all ganged up to use our legs to try to stop him. A fine way to relax before a great lasagna dinner.

Then yesterday, Monday, Becky, Danny, and I drove down the Coast Highway to Santa Cruz and visited the UCSC campus. It's up in the mountains above the city, so it looks out over the entire coastline of gigantic Monterey Bay. There are all sorts of redwood groves, just like Mill Valley. We met a professor who was a friend of Dad's and had a good time talking and even drinking some wine. I really want to go there and he was very encouraging. Becky liked it too. Danny doesn't want to go on to college just yet, but he took it all in too—the beautiful campus, the incredibly interesting faces, the warm afternoon sun cooled just enough for comfort by the afternoon sea breeze.

Next we crossed over the coastal mountains to Palo Alto and saw Stanford. It's beautiful too, but kind of overwhelming to me, too much like the Ivy League. I don't want that kind of pressure. Still I fantasized about how great it would be to visit Gloria there for weekends.

Finally, over the San Mateo Bridge and up the East Bay to Berkeley and another beautiful, magnificent campus, but a little too big and imposing for me. Becky, though, just about flipped out when she realized how much good music there was at both Stanford and Cal. I think she's starting to get more ideas about coming out here to college too. We had just enough time to take a ride on the bay from Berkeley on the hover-craft too!

Oh, I just have to mention a great game I discovered with Danny at the beach the other day—ultimate frisbee. It's played like touch football except it's passing only, no running with the frisbee. There's lots and lots of running too, with very long passes and lots of wild action. I can hardly wait to teach it to Tom and Joe and all the other guys.

Tuesday, August 8, 1989, Cotuit, MA.

I'm back on Cape Cod, back in all the normal summer routines again. California seems like another planet. I just read over A "HARD" DAY AT THE BEACH. If someone read it, they might get the idea I think about nothing but sex. I don't. I just leave out a lot of the boring stuff. Still, if Gloria were more available, I might not seem to be such a sex maniac.

I'm still angry at Gloria. Everything started off fine, as is usual when we haven't seen each other for a while. Playing around in California was fun, but I really missed her and wanted to spend a lot of time together and, of course, have sex as much as possible, which is never all that much. On about the third day I asked her up into the loft. I was particularly turned on to her because we had only made love once so far on this visit and hadn't spent more than an hour by ourselves the rest of the time. No big deal, really, just a lot of friends around. She likes to do stuff with Becky too, and one night we had to go to the Masterson's annual clambake where we ate and drank so much we immediately passed out afterwards. So naturally I expected today we'd slip off to the barn at the first possible chance.

Was I wrong! When Gloria said she wanted to stay up a while more and talk with Becky and a couple of their local girl-friends downstairs at the main house, I got annoyed, rightfully I thought. After all wouldn't any healthy, all-American guy want to make love with his girlfriend?

"Gloria, if not tonight, then when the hell *are* we going to get together?"

"You don't own me, you know. Remember our agreement from earlier this summmer. It takes two to tango, you know. It's not just a question of *your* needs."

A wave of fear zapped through my gut. Another heavy-duty proclamation about to come from Queen Gloriana! "Okay, let me have it. What's the matter *this* time?"

"I don't like your attitude, you nerd, but I will say it anyway. I'm fed up with being the only one responsible for birth control. I do not like inserting that foreign object into my body. I do not like to go out and get the cream for the diaphragm every time I'm going to have sex. Some men *do* put on the cream, you know. And then having to keep that "beige beauty" in there for at least six hours, and then I have to deal with a milky white discharge. And I'm supposed to check the expiration date of the cream. And remember to get a new diaphragm if it wears out and allows water to drip through. The pill made my whole system go WHACKO. I bled for a month with an IUD."

"Gloria, I've *told* you a dozen times that I'm more than willing to use rubbers."

My answer only caused Gloria to break down and cry. "I want to avoid an abortion if I can. We've been lucky so far."

I held her for a while, and then she left to see Becky and her friends. As I thought more about it, I couldn't blame her for being bummed. Why were we making something supposedly a lot of fun into something so heavy? I felt sympathy for Gloria for having to think about such stuff all the time.

For once I thought it might be good to have a little space from each other. Despite my sympathy, I was still somewhat pissed. And then, a couple of hours ago, over in Granny's house, Gloria and her mom were having one of their wild arguments. I heard Gloria shriek out, "If you tell me how to live my life any more, I am not going to put up with it. What works for you won't necessarily for me, you know." Val sounded as if she were staying pretty cool—she talked so much more softly than Gloria I couldn't hear her. But I think it might have been the pregnancy thing again because I heard the phrase, "ruin your career before it's off the ground."

Okay, I'm for a truce. If she wants her freedom, I can also get to do what *I* want without any guilt. I mean how many guys have that—and I think I'm safe with her anyway.

Now I know why I like to write up my life like it's a novel—the process somehow reminds me to have fun, not to take life so seriously.

Sunday, August 13, 1989

LIFE WITHOUT GLORIA

Casey was glad Mark was back. The recent flare-ups with Gloria, though they were perhaps necessary, created a heavy atmosphere that made Casey long for the simplicity of his California days. Birth control and possessiveness were, he admitted, issues almost every heterosexual relationship had to address, but for the moment, he was perfectly satisfied by being high on Mark's presence.

Mark would be around until Labor Day, that sad, sad time when all the summer folks packed up and returned to the suburbs. Until then, three more weeks with Mark around seemed fine to Casey. Luckily, Casey's family had little difficulty with Mark's bursts of wild energy. (Chuck loved to joke about what a yuppie Mark would be at thirty.)

It was Saturday morning, a beautiful, sunny day following two dull, overcast ones. After one of Sally's great blueberry pancake breakfasts, Casey announced to his folks, "Mark and I are going to visit his Aunt Mary on the Vineyard. We'll catch the ten-thirty ferry out and take the last one back, so we'll probably be having dinner at Mary's."

"Okay, fellows. Be sure to help her with the dishes."

"We will, Mom. She likes to cook for us anyway."

And so the guys caught the ferry, got picked up by Aunt Mary, and were given her car to use for the day. Aunt Mary, a very independent woman of about fifty, with little patience for "stuff and nonsense," lived in a beautiful, large white traditional Cape Cod-style home with another woman named Helena, who was away for the weekend. Mary had been married and divorced and had become much closer to her younger sister, Val, since the divorce. Casey had once asked Mark about the relationship between Mary and Helena, but he typically shrugged his shoulders, indicating that they could be lovers, could be anything, and that he didn't really give a damn one way or another.

Then the boys zipped westward all the way across the beautifully wooded interior of the island to the huge, wild beach on the Vineyard's west coast. It was more or less a nude beach, although not officially. The place was so vast and so few people hiked in more than a mile or so that you could pretty much do as you wanted.

They arrived there about noon, the sun glistening on the glassy ocean. They hauled in their beer and beach paraphernalia some two miles to a deserted area, found a suitable sand dune for their headquarters, took off their clothes and immediately started guzzling beers. Soon they dozed off.

A half hour later they awoke hot and sweaty, ready for a swim. Just after diving in the cold water, they looked up to see two young women approaching their encampment. They chose a sand dune about fifty yards away and also took off their bathing suits. No tan lines! One woman was blonde, the other a redhead. They greeted the guys with a wave as they too dove into the surf a few yards down the beach.

"I'll take the redhead, if it's okay with you, of course," Mark blurted out just before he plunged back into the surf. "Or must you remain faithful to Gloria?"

"The blonde's fine with me," Casey responded after Mark surfaced. "They both are fine; they seem friendly too. Hell, you know Gloria better than that. She won't mind. She encourages us *both* to have new experiences."

As all four emerged simultaneously from the surf a few minutes later, Casey yelled over to the new arrivals, "Anyone in the mood for a beer?"

"Sure," the two called back, and the four of them merged into a quartet of chatty exuberance. The women said they had some food they'd love to share with the beer and invited the fellows over to their dune.

"God, I'm hungry, let's eat. Weed, anyone?" asked Mark.

"You bet," said the redhead. "My name's Adrienne."

"I'm Leslie. Have a sandwich," said the other.

As the first joint began its merry course around the circle, Leslie and Adrienne indicated that they had just finished their freshman year at an experimental college near Boston. Casey and Mark reluctantly admitted that they were only going to be high school seniors. But, apparently, Leslie and Adrienne were not put off by younger men.

While chatting, they all discovered mutual acquaintances in Boston and soon started feeling good being together. Casey was happy with Mark's decision, for Leslie was relaxed and easy-going in addition to being attractive. Already he and she were lightly touching each other's legs and feet in the sand.

Meanwhile Mark and Adrienne had even more obviously paired off. They were holding hands and talking in an animated fashion. Casey couldn't help notice that Mark's cock was having a positive response. He then noticed that he too was also responding. But now for the awkward part. Which couple was going to move to the other sand dune?

It didn't really matter to Casey; he was just uncomfortable with the awkwardness of their all having to arrive mutually at a decision. Trying to be honest with himself, he noticed he felt a weak, but still weird, impulse of wanting them to all stay together in this dune. He hated the artificiality of one couple's having to walk off, as if they were involved in some kind of heavy ritual. It weakened the spontaneity of the whole fantasy. But he also assumed that not only the women, but probably Mark too, needed some privacy. So to make things easier for everyone, Casey invited Leslie to the other dune. She nodded okay, and Mark and Adrienne smiled good-bye.

Back at the original dune, Casey and Leslie relaxed and chatted amicably for fifteen minutes or so. After all he didn't want to come on like an obsessed sex-fiend. Soon, however, easily and naturally, the touching began. First there were some kisses, then some holding, both of them enjoying the warm surges of desire intensified by the romantic atmosphere of the wild ocean seemingly rooting them on. But then Casey's mind intruded with the thought that he shouldn't have intercourse with Leslie, probably because he was still bummed out about the issue of birth control. He had some condoms on him and could ask her what precautions she took. He decided, finally, he'd definitely prefer "safe" sex because he didn't want to break the mood by bringing up the subject.

Casey was happy just being close to Leslie, free to explore her body, kiss her lips, and touch her beautiful breasts. Soon, he found the idea of oral sex extremely appealing and Leslie seemed encouraging. In the next few minutes, she responded with her first orgasm. Her hands reached down to play with his cock. Then she surrounded it with her warm, moist mouth. After the better part of an hour, both contented, they dozed off together.

When he awoke, Casey could see that Mark and Adrienne had also dozed off. Casey had snuck a look at them earlier and saw that they weren't having intercourse. Since Mark's rubbers were in his pack in this sand dune, Casey was relieved at their caution.

Casey thought it was time to rejoin their friends. Leslie smiled and whispered, "Thank you, Casey," and put her arm around his shoulder as they returned to her dune. He felt relieved, somehow, when they were all together again, as if the party atmosphere had returned, not that he hadn't enjoyed himself with Leslie. But he was also curious about and attracted to Adrienne, too. And it had been so arbitrary, splitting into twos they way they did. Yes, it was great to smoke another joint with the whole group, to sip on a beer without a care in the world, now that that old demon "Horniness" was appeased for a while.

After another invigorating swim, all four wandered back to the women's dune and stretched out flat on their backs, faces into the sun. As Casey dozed off, he thought about Mark and himself, about how close they used to be, even closer than now. They never had to talk very much; there was just something electric in the air between them all the time. He thought back to the two-year stretch, beginning when they were thirteen, when Mark and he started messing around sexually together. He had mixed feelings about it now. He knew that it had been the danger Mark felt, especially about the other guys finding out about it, that had sometimes turned Mark on. Now, three years later, Mark seemed driven to prove his masculinity, probably as a way to gain the approval of the very same guys who'd be mortally offended if they ever found out he'd had sex with Casey.

As Casey sat up to take another hit of beer, he saw that Mark was leaning against a rock, legs stretched out, his whole being totally open and full of life. The good feelings flooded back into Casey as his love flowed to Mark in gratitude for the way he could enjoy life. Then Casey wanted to hug them all, Mark, Leslie, and Adrienne. He had a momentary fantasy of inviting them all some day to share in some kind of new-age family or something. At that moment, he was in fact slightly drunk, becoming a love-nut, enjoying one of those golden moments when dreams and fantasies seem within reach.

Then all four of them ended up at Aunt Mary's for dinner. After they had cleaned up, they took the ferry back to Buzzard's Bay. They exchanged addresses and phone numbers, although Casey figured such beautiful women must have steady boyfriends. Probably, like him, they had needed a change of pace.

Back at Cotuit, he was a bit of a bastard to Gloria. He and Mark couldn't help tease her by bragging with innuendos about their fantasy-come-true experience. Gloria pretended to be unconcerned, but Casey could see she was pissed. Secretly, he was kind of glad, but then his smugness immediately began to be tainted with guilt. He resolved to be extra nice to her, no matter how she acted during the next few days.

Sunday, August 20, 1989

That nice, quiet, Sunday night feeling. Dad's just left, giving Rob a ride back to New York City. Rob managed to get a couple of days off from his summer job, so he came up Wednesday night and at least got four days out of the city.

I'm not sure what to say about his visit. Rob's very different from me. There are a lot of ideas we share, but it's not as easy to share good times with him as it is with Mark. Rob talks a lot more, about books, movies and current rock music. That's okay. I do get a lot of good ideas from him.

I'm definitely going to take that seminar on Jung with him this fall. I'm not sure what all that stuff is about, except that Rob keeps mentioning how every man has an anima or inner woman and every woman has an inner man or animus.

What scares me about Rob is the fact that he's gay and that he digs me. This weekend, we spent a lot of time together, and, while he tried not to crowd me, he definitely wanted to spend as much time as possible together. He stayed up in the barn with me. We never touched at all. We were both being very careful, but I hate being that uptight together. Outside the barn, however, he always seemed to have a hand on my shoulder or to be casually bumping into me. And then I don't like the way he's so apologetic. I get tired of his putting himself down with comments like, "I wish my life were as together as yours", and stuff like that.

We did have great beach days at Wellfleet with all the neighborhood kids. Each of us drove out a station wagon full of noisy kids. It's strange to be one of the "big people" driving to Wellfleet, after being one of those kids for so many years.

Saturday after the beach, both of us wanted to clean up before dinner, but I knew the hot water was about to run out since both Becky and Chuck had just taken showers. Impulsively, remembering what we kids always used to do a few years ago, I offered to share a shower with Rob. We were kind of crowded in there—Rob's so big compared to Mark or Danny. After a couple of minutes, Rob's cock started getting a little hard. He was obviously embarrassed and turned away. I acted as if nothing was happening. A few moments later he seemed to arrive at the same conclusion. He turned around and faced me directly, as if to say, "What's to hide? I'm going to flow with this energy." What he actually said was, "Strange things are happening," an expression I had often heard him use before.

I looked him in the eyes, partially to pretend I didn't notice his cock, and said, "I'm really glad you're here this weekend," to show him I wasn't offended. He gave me a slight grin, relieved that he had "come out" to me with no negative consequences. I actually was a bit scared, so I started some cheerful, trivial conversation as if to say, "I can't really deal with all of this now, but I make no judgments and still want to be friends."

After I relaxed for a couple of minutes, I realized I was starting to get just a little hard. Before I could panic, Rob offered to wash my back. I agreed only because I got an excuse to turn around. After about ten seconds I offered to do his. His shoulders are so broad, his back had such a rocklike sturdiness. Then we lost ourselves in scrubbing and rinsing ourselves, finishing up just as the last of the hot water gave out.

Later that night, believe it or not, I talked to Dad about the incident on our walk to the grocery store. I told him I was scared of Rob's physical attraction to me and the implied expectations.

"See what a mess *your* open-mindedness has got me into," I accused.

Apparently what I said was funny, because Dad just laughed at me like I didn't know anything.

"Rob's a fine guy. You're very lucky—lucky to have a friend with so many fine qualities and lucky that he—and people in general—think you're attractive. Just think of Pat and me when you start freaking. If Rob's worth anything as a friend, he'll be happy no matter what you decide. Also, remember, you chauvinist, his getting turned-on is just like *your* getting an erection near a woman you're attracted to. You know, on the days I'm really down, I'm incapable of that sort of erection, the kind that's from being high on life."

"So how many months has it been since you've had an erection?" I sassed back, getting a good laugh out of it. Ol' Chuck smiled confidently, though. He was obviously in a strong area of his sexual ego.

Later, yes, I admitted to myself that I liked the openness of Rob's sensuality. Underneath his intellectual, "good boy" image was another vital, red-blooded American boy like myself—except he's gay. I also admitted I do kind of admire Rob for letting himself get hard. I mean when Danny and I did the same thing in California, it *was* fun. Or did the girls feel the way I felt a little with Rob, sort of turned off by being turned into an object? I guess that's why Dad said I should feel good about it. Hell, obviously he doesn't think there's anything wrong with desire in general or the way either I expressed it towards the girls or the way Rob expressed it to me.

Oh, I also talked to Rob a lot about going to college on the West Coast and trying to somewhat support myself. He had been headed towards the Ivy League, but he said maybe he'd apply to Stanford and Berkeley. I gave him some literature on UCSC, too. We both agreed it would be a big bonus to stay reasonably close to the Bay Area. "I know San Francisco's no New York," Rob said, "but at least it has good music and movies. I wouldn't miss my family all that much either and that's an understatement."

This afternoon, a nasty rainy day, we just sat around the barn reading and then rapping. Rob communicates so well; I feel so close to him, the way we share minds. You'd never go stale around him because you'd learn so much. Yes, I'm definitely attracted—at least to his mind. And, yes, his curiosity and vitality too. He's started being interested in UCSC. I had thought I made a mistake at first, thinking I might want to be on a different campus. That was definitely paranoia. I don't think I can handle sharing the same living quarters, but I do want to be on the same campus as he. It's funny about his friendship with Dad. That actually helps me trust Rob a lot more.

Friday, August 25, 1989

No doubt about it. There's a twinge of fall in the air tonight. The day dawned crisp and clear, with dayglow blue water on the bay. Some of the scrub oaks are already starting to change colors; it's the beginning of the long Cape winter. In the afternoon, dark clouds drifted over and the temperature never got above 65 degrees. Tonight is so cold that we built a big fire early, before dinner even, and it burned all night until half an hour ago when the family retired. It was so nice just to relax with everyone in the big living room which we hardly ever use up here.

Mark's still here, but Gloria's gone again. Right now I'm admitting that there's not an awful lot of interesting people around here for her. She leads her own life, going back home to Hastings occasionally to see friends there and then to Boston for shows, shopping, and more friends up there. In fact, I think Gloria's invited down some of that group for Labor Day. That'll be one monstrously chaotic weekend.

Val made it up again for a while, and I'm glad she did. We had a great time talking and sipping on mulled wine around that roaring fire. She kidded me about how the the easy part of my life was almost over, about how I wouldn't be able to coast in college as I do in high school, about how I'll have to study much harder. College will "shake you up a bit," she concluded.

Val looked great tonight, really young and mellow. She's been so sweet to Gloria and Mark, but she's one tough lady when she's working either on her financial business or political stuff. Like Mark she's tall and thin, but like Gloria she can look really stunning in those classy dresses she wears when she commutes to work. Tom and Joe hinted they thought she was a "dyke." First I just gave them my hard stare. Then I retaliated, "That's *her* business. But *whatever* she is, I think she's great." End of conversation.

Later, I pried Gloria about her Mom's sexual identity. Gloria seemed to regard the issue as trivial. "Oh, Mom's open to *any* good relationship. She's putting a lot of energy into us kids and into her career. I think her next big romantic relationship will come in a couple of years, after Mark and I have finished high school." End of conversation.

Anyway, after dinner tonight, we all gathered around the fire just to chat. I, as usual, played the devil's advocate, encouraging both Chuck and Sally to work less and to let themselves have more fun.

"You know, " Sally responded, "before I met Chuck I was so guilty if I ever had any fun, a typically self-sacrificing teacher, no doubt. Chuck has changed all that. He so obviously wants *all* of us to be happy. So now I insist on just the two of us taking a trip to the Bahamas each winter. As for summer happiness, all it would take for me is for both Casey and Becky to do a few more chores around here. Otherwise the Cape becomes a drag for me—as if I'm supposed to 'regress' to being an indentured housewife or something."

"I promise I'll be better," said Casey, trying to be cheerful and not wince at Sally's complaint, "because I don't want you becoming a workaholic like Dad. You know, Dad, sometimes you get so strung-out from work that you're too out of it to have *any* kind of fun with us. You could learn a lot from Mark about living in the moment."

"Indeed," said Mark. "How about trying out this joint. It's a great aid to living in the moment, at least until you go blotto—and then a blissful obliteration of consciousness."

"Ha, my dear son," Val responded, "perhaps there's a bit of a generation gap. One still needs to find a balance. Beware of too much fun or you'll feel worthless when you're older if you haven't accomplished something. I speak, of course, from experience."

"C'mon Val," Casey countered, "Mark's only sixteen. There's plenty of time for that work-ethic stuff."

"Yeah, Casey, even an old killjoy like me can go along with that," said Chuck, slightly offended, but still, trying to be a good sport. "Teenagers should have interesting lives, especially outside the prison of high school. The only caution I advise, as you all know, is to learn how to be unobtrusive around the people you might bother. That's been my biggest fear as a parent—how to teach kids not to get into trouble for values I approve of, but which most of society doesn't. With a little tact and a good sense of intuition, you can live any way you want, even in a Westchester suburb."

"Amen," Val assented. "I would have disagreed with you vehemently a few years ago, but you're right. It's the little hassles that wear you down while trying for political reform. We *need* to enjoy life just to stay sane."

"Speaking of enjoyment, Sal, what's that great smell?" Casey demanded.

"Val and I made a couple of berry pies for dessert," Sally explained. "Honestly, Casey, you looked eight years old when you asked that question, exactly as I first saw you," she smiled. "But, now, as fellow mature adults, in exchange for these delicious pies, you'll have to put up with us dessert chefs listening to the Boston Symphony broadcast tonight—Sir Colin Davis is conducting Mozart and Berlioz."

We all laughed at Sal's trying to bully us a bit. She's so giving and easy-going that she becomes even more appealing when she speaks up for herself. Yeah, they're a great family. You know it just struck me how lucky I am—to be able to enjoy spending some time with my parents socially. The last time I was at Joe's, I had to endure, after his father's second "cocktail", the usual anti-black, anti-Puerto-Rican and anti-faggot speeches from Joe Sr. while his mother quietly put up with it. If the guy wasn't so pathetic, I'd argue with him, but it probably wouldn't do any good. Anyway, I'd better adjust to him because I can't do without his wife's incredible pizza.

Sunday, September 3, 1989

What a wild holiday weekend it's been! Practically everybody's been here—Pat and Eddie, Mark, Rob, Tom and Joe, and Gloria for a while. And now we're packing to leave for school in a couple of days. I think I'll become Casey the novelist to try to put it all in some kind of perspective.

LIVE AND LET LIVE

Casey had been enjoying Pat and Eddie's visit for the last few days. It was always more fun when they were around. Eddie had just got some time off from his work so they could stay "for the duration." In fact, lucky them, they were going to stay on somewhat longer, into the Cape's usually beautiful September, until Pat had to return to his teaching.

Pat is Chuck's age. He is 5′10″ and wiry, with a young face and really clear blue eyes, despite his almost completely white hair. He talks quickly, in a very animated fashion. Or used to. In the last year or two he talks slower and less often. He's rarely gets angry, although he'd always say "we are not amused" when he took care of Casey as a kid and Casey did something stupid.

Eddie's taller and heavier than Pat, with somewhat curly reddish-blonde hair and freckles. He had a very difficult background and got addicted to coke, free-basing I think, in his early twenties. He always kids that he was "buffeted by fate," before he met Pat. Actually, he probably matured a lot after kicking the habit.

Needless to say it was strange having not only Pat and Eddie around, but also Tom and Joe— and Rob too.

Casey had always been a little uneasy when Tom and Joe were around Pat, since they had always badmouthed gays so much. Actually, this was the first time Tom and Joe had met Eddie. Casey thought that it might help if they were able to get to know some real gays casually. Casey figured it might be quite a positive education for Tom and Joe. At the time he had no idea how wild everything would become.

It all started late Saturday morning. Casey and Rob had driven over to Osterville to play free-style frisbee on the beach while the tide was low. He and Rob practiced tossing the disc whenever they had a chance so that both of them could throw it very well. Today they were making each other run a long way for just about every catch. Casey felt like a labrador retriever. His mind was almost completely turned off as he yielded to the sensations of the warm sun on his skin and the hard sand and cool, salty water beneath his feet. Every now and then, they'd throw the whirling disc a few feet into the ocean, giving each other the chance to cool off by making diving, spectacular catches as they hit the surf.

All of a sudden two more cars appeared, including Joe's Chevy. Out jumped Joe, Tom, Mark and a half a dozen of the local guys from Cotuit.

"Time for a game of ultimate," bellowed Mark. Casey had taught him and some of the other guys how to play after he had come back from California and now it was catching on. "Let's choose up sides and get going."

The energy level was very high, with all the guys wanting to run wild, competing for glory. Casey got totally swept up into their enthusiasm.

Tom and Mark had taken the responsibility of choosing up sides. As they did so, Rob whispered to Casey, "I don't want to play. I can't stand team sports. Can I have the car keys?"

Just then, before Casey could respond, Mark pointed to Rob and said, "You're on my team, Rob. Casey—you're with Joe."

"Count me out," said Rob. "I'm not any good and I don't like team sports."

"Hey, man, we need you to balance the teams. Do you want us to play with one team having an extra player?" Joe argued, possibly enjoying putting pressure on Rob.

"No way," said Rob. "I'm just not into it."

At this point just about all the guys had wandered up to form kind of a semi-circle around Rob. "Let the goddam sissy go," Tom tried to sound as if he were really disgusted.

Casey's mind was reeling. He was so hyped up for the game. Like Tom, he too, wanted even teams. He found himself saying, "C'mon Rob. Forget about the classical music and all the intellectual stuff for a few minutes. You can't believe how much fun it is to play with all the guys."

Casey will never forget the hurt look on Rob's face. But it was too late to take back what he had just said. Mark and the locals broke the tension somewhat by turning around and starting to chat with each other. Tom hung around, probably looking for more trouble, until Casey gave him a very dirty look, at which point he, too, turned around to say something to Joe.

"Just flip me the keys, please," Rob was practically begging. "Help me out of here."

"I'm sorry, Rob. That was *so* stupid of me. We'll talk about it later, okay?"

Rob said nothing in response, but simply caught the keys and walked away to the car.

Casey was relieved to see the car disappear. For the next two hours he lost himself in a great game of ultimate. Tom and Joe were very good players and their team did really well. Casey and Joe seemed to have almost telepathic communication. Knowing Joe was a powerful, accurate thrower, Casey would break away from his defender and run as fast as he could towards the goal line just as Joe caught a pass. Instantly Joe would launch a great throw that Casey had to run as fast as he could to snag the disc, many yards into the end zone, his defender a futile step or so behind. Joe and he were so hot that the other team couldn't stop the play even when they knew it was coming.

Afterwards they all jumped into the water for a dip even though the afternoon had become cool and overcast. Someone suggested getting cleaned up at the nearby Osterville Yacht Club since most of the guys had brought day packs with a change of clothes in them. They all trudged into the small, empty locker room feeling right at home since Casey's family, as well as the families of a couple of the other local guys, were members of the club. Somehow they all managed to crowd in. There were just two showers and no towels were supplied.

No one cared about any possible inconvenience. They were all the heroic gladiators, returning from their successful battles in the arena. Good feelings were rampant. It occurred to Casey that Rob in particular might really like this all-male world of occasional hugs around the shoulders and pats on bare behinds. The hot, steamy water felt so good. Tom did his usual exhibitionistic act when it was his turn in the shower, trying to be sexually provocative until Joe and Mark, pretending to be offended, both tried to pull him out, thereby creating an excuse for a free-for-all for a minute or so. Then, having all shared the single available towel, they hopped into their clothes, still somewhat damp, and jumped into the two remaining cars.

Casey ended up in Joe's Chevy with Tom and Mark. Still really high from the game, they decided to snack at a nearby Howard Johnson's where they sat in the padded orange booths and tried to stretch out their legs which were already stiffening up. But what a contented feeling of exhaustion! An hour passed, then two, as they all talked non-stop, mainly about sports.

As they drove back to Cotuit, Casey remembered that hurt look on Rob's face. He decided he'd immediately apologize to try to rid himself of an increasingly strong sense of guilt. But when he got to the barn, Rob wasn't there. There was a note, though.

Gloria invited me up to Boston to see a concert tonight. Back real late. Don't wait up.

Love,
Rob

Casey had to admit to himself that the word "love" relieved him. Rob couldn't be that angry at him after all.

"Casey, are you back?" It was Chuck's voice, down in front of the barn.

"Yeah, Dad."

"I'd like to come up and talk for a few minutes."

"Sure thing, Dad."

Casey heard Chuck carefully climb the steep rickety steps to the loft. As soon as he saw his Dad's face, he knew he was in trouble.

Chuck didn't hesitate. "Casey, I can't believe how insensitive you were to Rob today. At the very moment he most needed your support, you let him down."

"What's it to you, Dad?" Casey was suddenly furious. "I suppose he came to you like a cry baby after Tom called him a sissy."

Chuck simply glared at Casey whose fury suddenly evaporated, leaving him feeling defenseless. "Dad, I only meant to encourage Rob to try something new. It's not a hard game and he's such a good free-style player I though he might like it. I mean I can't tell you what an absolutely great time I had with the guys today."

"You picked a hell of a way to 'encourage' him, Casey. I, myself, sympathize with Rob because I also never played team sports very much. And the guys would turn on me, too, and accuse me of being a sissy or being 'queer'. It was traumatic, let me tell you. Can't you imagine how *terrible* Rob felt, trapped in that situation?"

"Damn it, Dad, gimme a break," responded Casey, almost pleading. "I already feel guilty enough as it is. I can understand that Rob needed you as a friend to talk to because he was so upset. But shouldn't your role in the matter end there? Don't you think Rob and I can clear this up on our own? You know, Dad, you have helped me develop a pretty strong conscience? Couldn't you leave me to punish myself?"

Chuck's look of parental disapproval softened to a relieved smile. "You've got a point there, Casey. And, yes, I can see your side, too. You simply wanted Rob to know what that feeling of being with the group was like. But I guess you realize that it's for Rob to decide. Lord knows there's plenty of ways to get some kicks out of life besides team sports."

"Agreed, Dad, if you promise not to meddle anymore."

This time Chuck just laughed and then held out his arms for a parting hug which symbolized the fact that all was well once again between them.

Later, after enjoying some time listening to music by himself, Casey's well-developed conscience began harping on him to confront Tom about his "sissy" remark to Rob. He climbed down from the loft and walked up the long driveway to the main house. Tom and Joe were just leaving by the back door, heading for the Chevy. Casey couldn't hear every word, but he could swear he heard Tom say, at one point, "Goddamn faggots."

Ignoring them momentarily, Casey ran up to the main house and looked in the living room window. There were Chuck, Sally, Mark, Val, Pat and Eddie all playing poker. Pat was taking in a very animated way and Eddie had crossed his legs tightly together. Surely Tom's "faggot" remark had been directed at them. Tom and Joe had had to pass through the living room to get from their upstairs bedroom to the back door.

Casey decided he had had enough. He caught up with the Chevy just as it was about to pull out of the driveway into Main Street. "Hey, I want to talk to you guys for a few minutes." Without asking, he opened the rear door on the passenger side and sat down, stretching out his weary legs on the back seat.

"C'mon along," said Joe. "We're just going out for a ride."

"Don't want to," said Casey.

"Well what *do* you want," said Tom impatiently.

"Tom, I'm sick of your attitude about gays. I thought that was a real cheap shot you made this afternoon to Rob. I was afraid you might be a little freaked about staying in the house with Pat and Eddie. But they're *good* guys. For God sakes, Eddie's even been playing touch football with us. My father's not gay and he's never played team sports. Don't you see how inaccurate your stereotypes are?" said Casey, hoping to confuse them about Rob's being gay. "Don't be so uptight. Live and let live."

Immediately Tom's eyes began looking weird. "Look, we don't like fags and we don't want to be around them. So what are you going to do about it?"

"Nothing, I'm going in the house to play poker. Look, Tom, you hothead, cool down. Joe, you seem to be the less prejudiced one. Try to talk some sense into his head. I can't force you guys to like gays, but if you're going to be my friends, you'll have to accept me as someone who does associate with gay people sometimes, which I'm going to do right this minute." Then, Casey immediately jumped out of the car and went back to the living room to play poker.

About a half an hour later, Tom and Joe returned. Pat immediately invited them to play and they said they would.

After a few hands everyone started to laugh, drink more beer and really get into the game. Casey was glad Tom and Joe each won big kitties after joining them; they were obviously losing themselves in the game. And there sat Pat and Eddie, totally oblivious to what had happened, simply enjoying themselves.

The game broke up about 1:30 a.m. Casey was exhausted, ready to pass out in the loft, face down into his pillow. But he mustered enough energy for a note to Rob which he tacked under the night light down at the bottom of the stairs in the barn. Rob would have to pass by it on his way to bed. The note read:

Dear Rob,

I'm sorry. Dad talked to me, but I was already very guilty. Please forgive.

With love,
Casey

PART II

HASTINGS-ON-HUDSON, 1989

Saturday, September 9, 1989, Hastings-on-Hudson, N.Y.

Back to boring old Hastings High. First, though, I never had a chance to write about the final days at the Cape. That brings up resolution number one, not to drink so much. All those parties did me in. I'd barely recover from one when it was time for another. Those old Cape Codders gave you plenty for dinner even though they called it hors d'oeuvres. Then you could handle even more of the best of the hard-core booze which they served. Of course we kids would also slip outside for an occasional joint too. A tough life.

But not as tough as the re-entry to "regular" life. How I hate the packing, the chaos, the rounding up of the cats. (Buzz just hid under the driver's seat. No problem.)

Now there's no more ocean, just a lot of homework and responsibility. I'm vice-president of the student council this year, a nice sounding title for college admission forms, but not much work—just a lot of boring meetings. It's good that student government doesn't take much time because all my courses have a lot of work. Just delivering the *New York Times* at school is enough of an outside job.

I've decided I'll work next summer at the Cape; at least I'll earn my own spending money. Dad and Sally both assured me that I should drop the paper route if it gets to be too much, but it's pretty easy. Besides I get around to every homeroom every morning, so it's a good way to see what's going on around school, especially to check up on the ever-exploding bosoms of certain sweet young things.

Hastings really isn't such a bad school. I'm currently being careful about how I behave lately because about a week ago I threw up running out of Miss Darby's class after I had won a ridiculous "chocolate cake" competition in the cafeteria against a couple of the football players. That damn Mark goaded me on. "C'mon, Casey, you *know* chocolate cake is your big weakness in life."

I like all my teachers except one, my composition teacher, Hartley Pompious. *Doctor* Pompious is what he makes everyone call him ever since he got his doctorate in education. He's a tall, stiff guy with steel-gray, very short, very neat hair who always wears three-piece suits and who has kind of an affected English accent. He *hates* me. He runs the class like a dictator and gave me detention the *first* day when I took advantage of a long pause to make one of my usual wisecracks. (I didn't even get detention for throwing up, although the vice-principal called me in to make sure that I apologized to Miss Darby. Of course, I swore I'd never do something that crazy again.) Everyone else in the class is terrified of him because he says that we're going to have to concentrate on grammar and take lots of tests before we'll ever have a chance to be good writers. We've had all that stuff before. It's just that everyone's so scared of him that they goof up when they write. I told Sally how awful he was, and she said that she's heard about him, that the other teachers don't much like him either.

I'm thinking of taking creative writing as an elective next semester, in addition to the required course in American literature. Dr. Pompious doesn't seem very supportive of such endeavors. He asked the class for examples of writing we do out of school. So I told him about this journal and how I sometimes experiment and write about myself in the third person as well as the first. He just stared at me for a minute and then said in a very sarcastic tone of voice, "Well, Charles, my precocious *wunderkind*, before you put yourself on the same level as James Joyce as an innovator, perhaps you'd best learn the fundamentals. I can just imagine all those clichés in your journal, all those dashes because you don't know the proper punctuation to use. We're here to learn—and *master*—basic, logical, expository prose."

I pretty much like my other classes, though. Hastings is a good school, with a lot of personal attention from the teachers. It's one huge, old red-brick building in the middle of town, so it's easy to reach for both the commuters' kids from the hills and the village kids. Every couple of years, the town votes against consolidation with neighboring Dobbs Ferry and Ardsley. It's more expensive to be small, but we want to stay on a personal scale. Sally feels so strongly about it that she campaigns like mad against the merger every time the issue rolls around again.

Sally also feels that the whole decade of the 80's hasn't been a good one for kids here—or anywhere else. We haven't had any suicides yet, thank goodness. But a lot of times, you'll see forty or fifty guys standing around the high school at night drinking beer, just getting out of their houses. There's more violence than there used to be, too, more fighting, as well as more group pressure to be tough-talking and tough-drinking, although there are still a lot of kids like myself who have fairly long hair and like literature, art, and classical music. We sometimes get teased, but I'm pretty much left alone by them.

That big group of drinkers almost never uses marijuana any more, although a small number of them fool around with more dangerous drugs—coke, speed, downers, etc. As for me, I almost never smoke pot at school—I'd rather save it for real fun outside of school. Besides, if you're caught, you get suspended immediately, and I don't want to embarrass Chuck and Sally—or have it on my record. Our neighbor, Paul, the assistant police chief, says that, all in all, alcohol is the destructive drug of the 80's—and that it's already nearly destroyed a bunch of kids right in this town.

Sally also says that she thinks it's a shame how so many kids in the middle school don't seem to have any sense of innocence left. She's right. I overheard two chubby eleven-year-old girls talking about "fucking," "sucking," "faggots," VD, and even AIDS as if they were the same kind of subjects as Nancy Drew and Michael Jackson. Sally says it's scary because they're so obviously media-influenced, dealing with the subject matter only on an intellectual level. "What is it going to do to their attitude about sex and romance when it's time for them to start dating?" Sally wonders.

Which brings the subject back to my sex life—or should I say non-sex life. Gloria is, in fact, *still* busy with all her stuff. So I've regressed to an old practice, beating off most nights before falling asleep. Usually, I fantasize about all the girls in a particular homeroom. Also, fond memories of Leslie and Adrienne—or even women I met out in California. Anyway I figure these hot, humid, end-of-the-summer days tend to intensify my romantic longings. (Stop rationalizing and pass the lube-tube.) I hope Gloria gets the school paper organized soon. Oh well, we're supposed to see each other tomorrow night.

Last night, the folks and Becky were out so I had the whole place to myself. I generally spend most of the time by myself in my room or down the basement in the rec room. But tonight, after a bath where I jacked off, I stretched out luxuriously on the long sofa in our living room and started beating off again to our huge-screen boob-tube (literally), channel flipping on the cable to check out all the lovelies, making up situations where I'd get to meet them, charm them, and then get to go off to some secret spot, usually outdoors, with them. Of course, they were always wildly turned on to me.

Probably millions of other American males were doing the same thing, sprawling on their sofas, with their pants down around their ankles, remote control device in one hand, dick in the other. We don't subscribe to the Playboy channel, but I've discovered that the picture doesn't scramble for the first second or so. So I keep madly flipping back and forth with the Christian channel to see some of the better boobs on the tube. Sometimes MTV is hot, too, but, mostly males, and I don't like any of the violent undertones.

It's weird that many typical guys are endlessly watching sexy, bare-chested, long-haired male rock stars on MTV.

Yesterday, back at school in the shower room with all the guys, it reminded me that we're all growing up fast. Some of the guys out for football and wrestling worked construction or spent a lot of time with weights over the summer and have gained twenty to thirty pounds of muscle. A couple of them already have hairy chests, too. So I also started thinking about my own body when I beat off in the buff. I really don't care that much about big muscles, and if I turn out about as hairy as Chuck, well, I'd be about average. I guess my cock's about average too. It's obvious that Gloria still thinks I'm attractive, probably Rob too, so I can't be all that bad looking.

I got tired of idiot box fantasies and briefly started thinking about Mark lying naked on the beach totally laid back, legs spread, as his cock started stiffening. And then an easy jump from Mark to twin-sister Gloria—yes, Gloria, naked, with her legs spread out on the beach and me walking up to her and touching her anywhere I want, doing anything I want. Then I get super-hard, and she helps slide my cock inside her. And then she's suddenly one of the sophomores at school, then another, and then I come.

And then, after a snack, beating off a *third* time. By then I was sweaty again, hot and sticky. Everything became stale, flat. Afterwards, I just wanted to escape by going to sleep. Once a night is definitely enough. When I came the third time, the cum just kind of dribbled out. (I wonder how many times I could come?)

Egad. I just thought how horrible it would be if the wrong persons, like Tom and Joe, got their hands on this journal. Sometimes I think I should lock it up, but that's just for women in the old-fashioned days. Why should I be paranoid, anyway? Dad always says we're all entitled to our private thoughts and fantasies, as long as we don't act out anything violent or harmful to others.

Still, I could be humiliated, so I am going to be a bit careful about keeping this away from curious eyes. Pat still keeps a journal, and he once offered his for me to read. And then he winked and said, "Maybe we could even exchange them someday and learn about each other."

Friday, September 15, 1989

I was in a bad mood today after reading all about yesterday's massive oil spill in the *Times*. Just seeing pictures of the poor birds caught in it made me furious.

And then, there's the situation with Gloria. It's not particularly to my liking at the moment. In fact it sucks. Case in point—a quickie note from Gloria yesterday:

Dear Casey,

I'm sorry I've been so busy lately. I do love you and do miss you—you are a wonder of male sweetness. However, I am now in a phase of growth when I sometimes find you too intense about our relationship. I need to have other experiences too, especially with my new women friends in Boston, whom I unfortunately won't get to see very often this semester. Yesterday, I accepted the offer of a date from Donnie Wilkins for tomorrow at the movies. You shouldn't be worried or jealous; things need to run their course. I know we both enjoyed our freedom this summer, and I do think our allowing ourselves this freedom is currently one of the best things about our relationship. You're too serious sometimes about things, and I need to try being just light and frivolous with another guy. Besides, do you know of any other boy-girl romance that's trying to, as Mom would say, "sift out the symbiosis" before it causes trouble later? I didn't think so.

So my dear, sweet, wonderful Casey-kins, my luscious-tasting, not-junk-food-at-all, tasty Casey-cakes, accept the love I feel for you right now. It's you, you, you who I really love, but I've always wanted to date Donnie, so may I indulge my whim? If you can't give me your blessings, at least put up with me.

Love and kisses,
Gloria

What can I say? I'm having these nasty thoughts about what a shithead Donnie is to ask her out. And then endless thoughts where I compare myself with Donnie over and over in every possible way—I'm taller, he's stronger, I'm smarter, he's more charming, etc. He's definitely better looking, dammit—there's no question about that. I keep hoping they won't have any fun, or that one of them will get sick and they'll have to cancel it. And my thoughts about Gloria are the lowest of all. "I bet she wants to become sexually promiscuous," I thought, as if I had exposed a horrible side of her, "She probably *asked* him for the date."

Then I heard Dad's voice in my mind saying, "C'mon, Casey, you've played around a bit. That's fine, but it's also fine for Gloria. She's not doing anything rash, and she's not secretive. That letter was the total truth."

So I went and chatted with Sally, playing out my need for sympathy. And good ol' Sal gave me a lot, although it was more "for all the trials young people must face" rather than for me in particular. "Poor Casey. All you kids think you have new values, but you will soon find out how painful adolescence and young love usually turns out to be." I realized her nurturing was fine for me in my state, but not her attitude about the inevitability of pain accompanying teenage romance. I didn't want to accept her philosophy, yet I still lapped up all the love I could from those soft, brown, understanding eyes.

I went to my room and immediately got very stoned and started feeling depressed and sorry for myself. But then I remembered Pat's comment about using relaxation techniques to let out tensions, especially when you're stoned. So I sat down in the lotus position and chanted to myself, "You are not alone; you are ALL-ONE." At first, I was bored, but I forced myself to breathe deeply a few times. After a while, I alternated between feeling better while chanting and feeling paranoid while "obsessing" about Gloria and Donnie. I gave up after a few minutes, but I felt pretty good. An hour later, I slipped back into being angry and jealous, but at least I found out I had this technique to help me a little if I get too freaked out.

Friday, September 22, 1989

BOYS WILL BE BOYS

Casey was off to his usual slow start at school. (Pompious gave him a "C" on his first paper, the first such grade he had ever received in English.) Assignments were short at first, and, while he might have started reading or research on any number of projects already assigned for later in the semester, he was too restless to stay home by himself this particular evening. He had seen Gloria once since she had dated Donnie, and they had had a good time together after some initial tension. Casey had hesitated about asking her what had happened with Donnie, but she didn't volunteer much information. Then she disappeared for the weekend up to Boston, only to return "behind in my work." The best he could do was to plan a date for the following weekend.

So he resorted to going out once again with Tom and Joe, because Mark was out of town on a new daredevil episode, learning how to fly a hang-glider. Joe suggested cruising around East Yonkers and upper Mt. Vernon. Casey was scared by the prospect of getting into a fight with any of the tough guys from those blue-collar homes. Joe and Tom had been acting a bit nasty lately themselves and had even been bragging about how well they had done in a couple of recent scraps. They had both been really nice to him ever since he got pissed at them at the Cape.

Off they went in Joe's red Chevy, cruising first around Bronxville and then Yonkers. Casey, admittedly somewhat uptight, managed to talk them out of going to Mt. Vernon. Instead they turned up Central Avenue, the "strip" of southern Westchester County. With the tape deck blasting out good rock, it wasn't bad at all. They tried out the action at Watson's, but couldn't get in because Casey, unlike his companions, didn't have a fake I.D. Sometimes Casey could pass, no questions asked, but this place checked everyone, probably because it often got raided.

Still no place to go. So they cruised down Central Avenue some more and stopped at a drive-in to see what the younger crowd was up to. Casey couldn't believe he let himself get into this situation. Joe started talking to a group of four girls, probably about sixteen, a little tough, but nice. Soon they had all wandered outside of the car and were just rapping. Oh, one important detail—they were all pretty drunk. Tom had swiped a quart of rye from his father which he materialized when the beer disappeared, and now it too had vanished. Casey shuddered to think that they'd had much more than he and he was pretty shit-faced. Well, it was fun for a few minutes as they all found out about each other and kidded about high school rivalries.

But then trouble when three guys got out of a parked car, one black, one white and one probably Puerto Rican, all of whom apparently went to the same school as these girls. Casey just wanted to jump back into the car as nonchalantly as possible and quickly drive away. Not so Tom and Joe. You could tell they were looking for trouble, that they wanted to fight. So they started needling these guys with put-downs, just verging towards racist comments. Casey tried jiving a bit on a friendlier basis, hoping to defuse the situation. But Tom, especially, wouldn't stop. The white guy seemed particularly incensed at the insults to his friends. "All you fags from Hastings," he taunted, "are just a bunch of rich fairies."

Tom suddenly rushed the guys, with Joe immediately following suit. Casey was first pissed at his friends, then suddenly afraid for them. Three against two: his male pride insisted he make at least some gesture to help his dumb-ass companions, so he advanced to be close enough to touch all the scufflers, but there he remained, paralyzed. He could only think in terms of slipping off to Joe's car to prepare a quick getaway from either more fighting or the police.

But he was too late. Apparently an onlooker had already called the police. The scuffle had no sooner started when three squad cars arrived. The fighting stopped immediately. One officer spoke through a bullhorn, "Okay you hoodlums. Nice and easy now. Line up. Don't move."

The rest of the policemen then proceeded to frisk them violently, handcuff them, and shove the six young men, including Tom, Joe, and Casey, into their patrol cars for the drive to the precinct station where they had to tell the usual information about date of birth, parents, addresses, and school.

Nothing to worry about, thought Casey; they're just looking for previous offenders. But he *was* worried.

When the cops discovered that the Hastings trio were outsiders, the boys had to listen to some harsh bullying about what would happen to them if they were ever again caught back in this city. After some more abusive verbal knocks from an obnoxious sergeant, another officer announced they'd have to notify their parents. Casey saw Tom and Joe wince, as they anticipated yelling and even possible beatings from their drunken fathers. Casey then had a practical idea. Rather than insisting on his innocence in the fighting, Casey volunteered to have his father come over to pick up all three of them. Reluctant at first, the officer agreed, but only with the stipulation that he, personally, would call Tom and Joe's parents later to inform them of the incident.

As soon as Casey was about to dial his own number, he remembered, with a sickening thud in his stomach, that Chuck and Sally were at that moment entertaining all these distinguished, professional types, planning some kind of benefit for charity. It was only eleven; most of the guests were probably still there. When Chuck answered the phone, Casey's heart dropped because he heard so many voices in the background. He tried to be cute. "Dad, if you know where Precinct #6 in Yonkers is, you can come claim three guys who very much need your services. At your leisure, I mean. I know there's a party going on."

"Casey, are you okay?"

"Tom and Joe got in a brawl on Central Avenue. We all got taken in. They'll release us when you get here."

"Okay, sounds as if it's no big deal. I hate to do it to you, Casey, but I need another hour here to talk to someone very important. He's leaving the country tomorrow and won't be back for six months. Then, when I'm finished with him, Sally can cover for me if the guests are still here."

Relieved, Casey explained to everyone that his father would be an hour or so.

"I guess you guys would like to know what it's like to be in a cell," said the obnoxious sergeant who instructed two of his patrolmen to lock them up. It was so classic—the spoiled, white suburban boys would be taught a little lesson.

Tom and Joe got put in an empty cell together, but Casey wasn't so lucky. His cell was bleak, just two cots and a john. His cellmate terrified him, especially when he informed Casey that "his cute white ass" would be very popular around this place. Casey figured he was only kidding, but felt violated anyway. He had to take a wicked piss after all that booze, but he couldn't stand the idea of his cellmate's watching him and then maybe making even more overtly sexual comments. The hour in jail seemed to last a whole night. Casey was so relieved when Chuck and the sergeant finally appeared to let him out.

They left the station and drove Tom and Joe to Joe's car. This time Casey was glad to accompany his Dad, for he knew from the past that Chuck had enough class not to rub it in too much. Off drove Tom and Joe, with Chuck and Casey following. For the first five minutes of the drive, neither of them spoke. Then Chuck broke the ice. "I'm betting you weren't at all involved in any fighting."

"No, I wasn't."

"So I guess you just like to hang around with those guys sometimes. I can't say as I blame you—I mean, theoretically, I've always said it's good to learn from a wide spectrum of friends." Chuck laughed good-naturedly at how his parental advice had backfired in this instance. Casey was not laughing. He just sat there stewing.

But Chuck wasn't about to let it drop. "Casey, I can't believe you could be so dumb. I've got nothing against Tom and Joe and I'm certainly not going to be so foolish to say you can't go out cruising with them any more since that'll only encourage you, but why do you do it? Why these guys? I'm starting to wonder if you like getting into trouble, maybe even causing me a little embarrassment."

Pause. "Not really Dad. You know that they're good guys and I enjoy hanging around with them. All the guys at Hastings I know are so serious about studying. These are my only friends from the village who aren't obsessed about college and their careers. I need the release."

"Release?" Chuck sounded annoyed. The tone of his voice became more authoritarian. "Release! Casey, I've been around long enough to know that thrills from violence and danger will always attract young men. I can't force you to be a pacifist if you haven't yet overcome such urges."

Casey fumed a bit because he felt Chuck should know that he *was* over such urges, that he already considered himself a pacifist. "Dad, basketball starts next month. Don't worry. That'll give those guys and me a constructive way to deal with those 'violent' energies as you call them."

"Well, I'll let your future behavior provide the credibility. You know I love you, even though I don't often spend enough time with you. Let's meet in the city and go out to a show or a basketball game or something really soon."

What more could Casey say? Chuck's guilt soothed Casey's hurts. As they approached their house, Casey patted his father's shoulder, then kind of grabbed it and said, "Thanks," not thanking him so much for the invitation, as for being so forgiving.

All the guests were gone when they arrived home. Sally gave Casey a warm, welcoming hug and he, in turn, grabbed Buzz and gave the startled feline a love-drenched squeeze. Then, Casey dumped Buzz out of his arms and quickly walked over to Chuck. Father and son embraced ferociously, instantly putting the incident behind them. Up in his bedroom, it was a very tired, very relieved Casey who passed out instantly the moment his head hit his pillow.

Saturday, September 30, 1989

I had to take Buzz to the vet today. About six this morning, I heard the murderous screeches of a cat fight. I ran downstairs and found Buzz in the backyard, his whole backside covered with his own ca-ca, looking totally traumatized. I cleaned him up as best I could, putting him on a towel in front of the fireplace. He seemed to be limping and so, afraid one of his legs was hurt, I took him to the vet.

"I've seen this before. He just got the shit beat out of him. I don't see anything that might possibly get infected, but keep an eye on him and let him rest up for a couple of days. If I were you, I'd have him neutered too. He'll still get into fights, but, as it is now, you risk serious injury, even a mortal wound, if he ever gets into a fight over a female in heat."

Is it in all male hormones to fight? I don't know, really. I guess it is on an animal level. People don't have to, though.

Monday, October 2, 1989

What a great night at the old Westchester homestead. Pat and Eddie were down for a visit Saturday night, and, since it was my birthday (seventeen!) they brought some goodies. Dad, Sally, Becky, Gloria, Mark and Rob were there too, and Sally made a super-huge vegetarian pizza. She also had lots of artichokes and avocados, my favorites, for the occasion. And we made home-made ice cream, both chocolate and banana.

After dinner, we all lounged around our living room, with the fireplace blazing away since the outside temperature had dropped very quickly after a warm, hazy autumn afternoon. These are my favorite times in our big living room, which is usually strewn with all the books and magazines all four of us are in the middle of reading. Pat and Eddie fit so naturally into our way of life. Earlier in the evening, I could see that Pat was wiped out from teaching and feeling angry at his administration—his face looked drawn, with lines tightened around his eyes and mouth. Eddie, who had had a day off from his woodworking, seemed fine. He told some more stories about what it had been like to be hooked on coke.

I have to admit all four of my parents are pretty sane about drugs. They try to limit Becky and me to *small* amounts of alcohol and marijuana. Sometimes, Tom and Joe have coke or speed, but I always turn it down. True, I've listened to Chuck's speeches about "circumspection" and "what's appropriate" all my life. It's Pat, though, who's pointed me in the right direction, telling us to use grass as a learning device, to raise consciousness rather than lower it. He even got Chuck into a little grass and meditation about five years ago as a way of helping him keep down his blood pressure.

About eleven, everyone excused themselves for the night except Pat, Eddie and Rob who were all staying over. At first we just quietly stared into the fire. Then Pat murmured something to Eddie about one of their friends who was paranoid that he might have AIDS. After some more silence, Rob asked Pat what it had been like to be gay before all the problems with AIDS. "I guess you could have done anything sexually you wanted to do without having to worry so much. It was more fun then, wasn't it?"

Pat winced, but didn't say anything. He looked perplexed. Eddie broke the tension, though. "It's not so bad now. You just have to be careful to avoid exchanging bodily fluids. Oh, I suppose using rubbers, too, if you want to check out anal sex. Don't feel you have to, though. The rectum is super-susceptible to disease, you know."

Now it was Rob's turn to look perplexed. He had tried to phrase his comment so it wouldn't sound like a personal request for information, but I'm sure Eddie wouldn't have been so explicit if he hadn't thought he had a chance to help Rob.

"I was just thinking," Rob went on, "it must have been great to live at a time when you could just enjoy yourself sexually—just do everything you wanted to do—without having to be paranoid. It must have been so great to have had that freedom to go wild without feeling that it could kill you."

Pat stared at Rob the whole time he spoke, then responded with a bittersweet smile. "No doubt young people deserve some kind of a phase of sexual exploration, Rob. But, back before AIDS, so many gay men got stuck in that phase—got obsessed with it, even. I can only speak for myself, but my karmic message about sex seems to be, 'Don't repeat experiences you've already had and lessons you've already learned.' It strikes me as so odd that you're curious, even envious, about the past. It seems to me AIDS has caused your generation to focus on loving principles for sex and relationships at a much younger age. From my perspective, that's a break for you guys. There's not so much time wasted aimlessly sleeping around."

"Yeah," agreed Eddie. "You can't act pre-AIDS in a post-AIDS world anyway. Why fight it?"

Rob didn't answer, but looked somehow relieved, as if some nagging question had been answered. His brown eyes sent out looks of gratitude to both Pat and Eddie.

Then, when we were all getting up to go to bed, Pat slipped me a small package. Later, I brought his gift upstairs, and, just before going to bed, I opened it and found this note:

Dear Mr. Wonder-Teen,

I think you'll find this little volume, Thaddeus Golas' A LAZY MAN'S GUIDE TO ENLIGHTENMENT, most handy for facing life's little perils and challenges. Use the GUIDE in good health. I particularly like it because it tells us to enjoy life, yes, but it also wants us to embrace "bummer" thoughts and moods as part of one's journey to enlightenment. Its section on how to use marijuana positively, for self-knowledge, should also interest you.

Dear, sweet Casey, may your next year be blessed in every way, and may you come to enjoy the harmony of inner and outer that is a Libra. Wing it. Use your airiness to fly above the world when it's all too much. And enjoy all the beauty and silliness of this world when you're truckin' along in your usual high gear.

Much love,
Pat

Monday, October 9, 1989

Wow. *The Lazy Man's Guide to Enlightenment* is great. I've already read it several times (true, it's only about eighty short pages). I've also been putting some of my favorite ideas on cards.

To begin with, I like the idea that we can raise our level of vibrations by remembering to love more often—that's expansion. But then in the usual cycles of life, we inevitably contract and become negative. But if you can "love yourself for where you are, right now, this instant," you start to expand again. "No resistance." That's one of his big ideas too. Just flow with life and you'll expand.

Here are three cards I posted on my wall to help me remember the ideas as much as possible:

1. Expansion in love is an action that is always available.
2. Your internal condition is never programmed.
3. It is precisely your unlimited power to control your experience that hangs you up. Just grant to others the freedom, love, and consciousness you want for yourself.

Heavy! I really love #3. It's exciting to believe that your vibrations do create your future. Still, like a good scientist, I need to test this stuff out, especially when the next bummer comes along.

Wednesday, October 11, 1989

Buzz is hurt again, another abscess, my poor little pal. We had to ship him off to the vet. Of course, he resisted the whole time. He's so independent; he hates to be helped by anyone. I can't stand to see him hurt; sometimes I wish it were me instead.

A couple of weeks ago, he missed his appointment to be fixed. He just disappeared for two days; I cried thinking that he was gone for good. Luckily, he showed up a couple of days later. We waited a bit longer, and then had it done last week. I guess there's no such thing as a pacifist male cat, but now that he's both fixed and reestablished for a month or so in his own home territory, maybe he won't get into any more fights.

Funny, Buzz loves to meditate with me. Everytime I go into the lotus position, he jumps onto my lap and quietly purrs in a regal posture. Or sometimes he'll sit in front of me like the sphinx, just beaming out highly evolved vibrations. Maybe it'd help if I'd get synched in telepathically with him when he's on my lap and tell him not to get hurt anymore.

Monday, October 16, 1989

THOSE GARDNER TWINS!

Luckily, Casey's room is virtually isolated from the rest of the house because when Mark comes over, they usually get stoned and play rock music *loudly*. All the rest of the family was out, so on this particular night, they even boomed the bass. Then Mark said he wanted to take a shower, that he felt grubby from playing touch football before dinner. He took off down the hall to the bathroom. Just before he left, though, the boys had broken out a bottle of Chuck's Jack Daniels.

Since they did this so rarely, Chuck usually didn't mind as long as they didn't abuse the privilege. They each poured themselves a half a tumbler over a bunch of ice cubes, and then off Mark went. Casey just sat there sipping, listening to the music, and fantasizing about meeting Gloria in this same room twenty-four hours from now.

Mark came back with his towel around him ten minutes later. First, he poured some more booze and put on the Stones. Then they smoked another pipeful of good weed Danny had just sent from California. Not surprisingly, they fell into a kind of trance, not talking, just listening to the music. Suddenly, Mark took off his towel, his cock almost stiff, and looked at Casey as if to say, "What are we waiting for? Let's beat the meat." And so he sat down next to Casey and started beating himself off.

"Mark," drawled Casey slowly, "I thought we weren't going to get into this sort of thing any more."

Mark didn't answer, but just kept jacking off. Casey hesitated, looked at Mark again, took off his pants, sat next to him on the bed and started beating off too. Something about Mark's nerviness was irresistible. He wanted to share that kind of "wicked" arousal. Mark then looked over at Casey, pretending some kind of innocent curiosity, then reached over and started beating off Casey as well as himself. Casey loved it when he closed his eyes, but when he opened them, Mark looked like he was having so much fun that he insisted on trying both of them too. Then Mark took over Casey's cock, but let Casey keep beating him off. Suddenly they were back in their groove, with good music and these rushes of good feelings for each other. They grabbed harder, pulled more, went faster and faster. Then they both came like volcanos—Mark obviously was as horny as Casey—then Mark left Casey his towel and took off once more for the shower, careful not to let the cum on his stomach drool down his leg. When he returned with his clothes on, Casey was also dressed, and they continued to listen to music, not saying much of anything.

What was happening? Was Casey, the typical, all-American guy, just regressing to an earlier phase? Or? Casey didn't want to go into the "or" for now, except to say that afterwards he was left with some feelings of resentment towards Mark. For bringing back the buried past? For playing games with Casey's feelings for him?

Then Gloria came over the next night, again to a peaceful, empty house. It was a perfect evening. Not only was Casey hot for Gloria, he honestly acknowledged to himself the urge to have a bona fide heterosexual experience after that previous night with Mark. Of course, once again he saw and enjoyed all the subtle physical resemblances between the twins—the lankiness, the different shades of skin and hair coloring, the shapes of their mouths, noses, bodies—what a rush, the comparisons drove him crazy with desire, especially since he knew he was here with Gloria now.

They started in with deep kissing. Then he rested his face against her neck. Suddenly, there was that warm rush of a feeling, loosely translated as "How happy I am to be close to you again." God, I love this woman, thought Casey, especially when she's so sweetly loving.

After that rush of energy, Casey started having naughty fantasies of being with *both* the twins.

But then Gloria started gently kissing his lips and Casey just lay back and enjoyed the present. It was wonderful— neither of them was in a hurry at all. (Actually, he thought the experience with Mark had helped calm him down. Gloria didn't understand that he needed some sexual release just about every day to, well, just keep him calm about it all. He guessed horniness was simply a part of life, even when you had the "perfect" girlfriend.)

Off together into the clouds they hugged for a long, long time and slowly got into giving each other a ton of pleasure. Casey totally enjoyed arousing Gloria for a long time. He could tell she was into it herself. One night he had heard Val lecture Sally and Gloria on how important it was for women to enjoy their own bodies. She seemed totally relaxed, so Casey kept stimulating her, truly enjoying her pleasure when she had her first orgasm.

"Oh, Gloria," Casey blurted out just as Gloria was returning from her enraptured state, "What about birth control?"

"Relax, silly. You can't get pregnant from masturbation."

"Yes, but . . . "

"I have an idea just for tonight. I don't have my diaphragm and I know you're not crazy about rubbers, so let's just do without intercourse for a single evening. That's not too great a sacrifice, is it?" she concluded in a flirtatious voice.

"Gloria, I think . . ." Casey started to defend himself but, catching on finally that she was teasing, he suddenly overpowered her with a big hug which pinned her prone to the bed. Then he started eating her with the same gusto he had felt earlier. Why wasn't his cock insisting on some attention? Who cares. He sure had the energy, and Gloria lay back and enjoyed herself. They switched to French-kissing again—then they started playing with each other while they still kissed. Their sense of pleasure and sharing was as intense as any previous experience. Gloria came a second time. Later on she came a third time, just as Casey exploded. Afterwards he felt so damn *good*—so relaxed, so peaceful, so agreeable.

Such closeness and love. Casey felt so *assured* of Gloria. He was momentarily glad she wanted to be independent and felt good about not needing her all the time anymore. Also about her not needing him all the time.

They felt so close afterwards as they held each other that he just had to relieve his mind and tell her what had happened with Mark the day before. She seemed sympathetic about the fact that Mark was mixed up. For some reason Gloria never seemed the least bit jealous of his feelings for Mark—or any other guy. How could she be so mellow? She actually gave him advice to help the situation. "If Mark and you are going to become closer emotionally, though, he's going to have to do some growing up. Then, too, Casey, it takes great courage to accept bisexuality these days. Be careful, you two. Well I guess the last thing you would do would be to advertise it. But don't confide to any of the other guys." And then she laughed and said with a gleam in her eyes, "At least with any of the guys you haven't yet had sex with."

Then a pause, a more serious look, while Casey remained silent. "Meanwhile Casey, thanks for the fantastic evening. Have I told you yet today how wonderful you are? I feel so *good* towards you ever since you've been able to give me more space. I'm realizing I can have my life *and* have you too. What a great feeling! Oh, by the way, with the holidays coming up, I'll be going up to Boston whenever I can to see my friends."

Casey felt a rush of anxiety sweep through the pit of his stomach. Why did Gloria ruin this perfect experience by bringing up her need to be independent? True, she did compliment him and that made him feel very good. Maybe he needed more of his own life too, instead of just waiting for her. He was tired of hanging out with the likes of Tom and Joe just to do something. Right now he'd love to have another lover, a relationship with another woman. Maybe then the great Gloria Gardner wouldn't take him so much for granted, he thought to himself, as they fell asleep in each other's arms.

Saturday, November 4, 1989

A very difficult evening after a self-indulgent day. I sort of pretended I was sick and stayed home from school and watched TV. I do have sore gums where a wisdom tooth is cutting through. Masochist that I am, I poked around it all day with my tongue even though it hurt.

I *think* I can explain last night. On the surface I'd say that I ate too many marijuana crunchies. I followed Pat's recipe and used up all my leftover shake by baking it with wheat berries and butter. But being sort of sick, I had skipped dinner and ended up so hungry that I ate half the whole pie, just out of the oven. What a mistake! At least I feel okay today.

I was just lying there after "ingesting the substance," thinking how great things were with Gloria and looking forward to the seminar on Carl Jung in a couple of weeks. All of a sudden, I felt this sense of terror. I wanted to open all the windows and let in some air. Everything was starting to spin, and I thought I might black out. So I started doing deep breathing which helped for a while.

When I stopped the breathing exercises, though, I realized that I was very, very stoned and was going to be very, very stoned for quite some time. I had just had a thought about Rob when the first rush of paranoia hit me. I started to cough, to gag, to get the dry heaves. There was so much fear in the pit of my stomach.

After about another ten minutes, guilt hit, especially guilt for enjoying sex with Mark a couple of weeks ago. All kinds of self-accusations—how I was too old to do that anymore, how it was disgusting. And then I tried to rationalize it. It was very infrequent, it didn't matter in the long run, it wasn't any big deal etc. But only more and more agonizing guilt. The only way I could calm myself down was to promise myself not to ever again have sex with a man.

But the freak-out continued. I compared myself to Dad and felt so lazy, so crummy, so spoiled, so useless. It seemed as if I only wanted the easy way in life—going to UCSC instead of competing in the Ivy League, not labelling myself "pre-law" or "pre-med", and not committing myself to some other meaningful career through which I could help people and repay my parents for having given me so much. I accused myself of being a slob, drinking too much, smoking too much weed, being dishonest, lacking integrity, especially in comparison to Dad and Pat, being sex-obsessed, and a whole lot of other shit. I felt selfish and self-centered (especially in comparison to Dad). Sally seemed like a saint—how could I be a match for her kindness and compassion?

I thought the worst was over then and that I was calming down, but I was wrong. The hum of the refrigerator and the tick of the clock both seemed super-loud as I nervously paced the house. Then a whole new set of attacks began. I had the sense that God wasn't happy with me at all, that something terrible would happen in the future to punish me for all the things I was doing. I thought I wasn't doing what God wanted me to do at all, that I was just doing what felt good and, again, being selfish, not helping the world, not using my life like Christ or the Buddha to help others.

Then I heard a defiant inner voice say, "And I'm not going to spend my whole life working to help others either, like that fool, Chuck." This thought only worsened my guilt.

Fears about God's judgment began to really hit me. Finally, I remembered that idea about vibrations, that maybe I should try to like this awful state I was in. I put on the Grateful Dead and tried not to think so much. That angry, scary God now seemed more like a product of my foolish imagination, but my imagination had been powerful.

So finally, much, much too late, I remembered that I had marked several passages in the *Guide* on what to do during a bad trip. An hour later, after a walk and more deep breathing, I could see that I had been overwhelmed by buried feelings that the large quantity of dope had released like a truth serum. I think that's why I feel so good today. I'm still confused about myself, but I feel lighter, cleaner, as if it'll all be worked out sooner or later.

I told Dad about what happened, not about the gay stuff. I'm still uncomfortable talking about that with him. I told him about the part when I criticized myself and felt worthless and selfish, that God thought I was messing up my life. His little speech helped.

"I think Pat would say that when you like yourself, you feel in harmony with God—it's all interconnected. I bet you were in a bad mood to begin with, maybe already sulking from playing hooky. You got overwhelmed by some self-hate, but you handled it well. Just don't take your thoughts seriously when you're bummed out. And, then too, maybe you do need to think some more about a career. And, for God's sake, lower your dosage!"

Pretty good advice, and yet I felt a surge of resentment at the end, especially at how slick his manner was, how smooth his delivery was when he said it, almost as if he were reassuring a client that he had everything under control. Yes, that's Dad. A great guy, but I've never heard him talk about his own bad trips.

Then I called Pat to talk about this stuff. He said that he's had many bad trips that, with some perspective, turned out to be necessary, even useful to growth. As usual, he was very helpful.

Friday November 10, 1989

It's Sunday night, following yesterday's first of six classes on Carl Jung's life and ideas. So far, I think the professor's great, and I like some of the students. We meet in a fancy seminar room at Columbia, all seated around a long, beautiful oak table in big, plush chairs. The group is about a dozen women, Rob and me and only a couple of other guys. Dr. Bronstein remarked that, "Young men are traditionally reluctant to try to see life in a Jungian perspective because they are afraid of their inner, emotional side, their animas."

It was also great seeing Rob. Even though I assume Rob's gay, I'd say he understands his anima, his feminine side, less than his masculine side because he lives so much in his mind. I think he also needs more love than his parents have given him.

I keep saying to myself that I want life to be simpler. This Jungian stuff focuses on complexity too much for me. I have decided to direct all my sexual energy towards women, and I mean to stick to that decision. It's as simple as that. When I look around me, every other heterosexual guy I know has made the same decision.

But then I meet a guy like Rob, and I get this sense of potential, that if we were ever able to have a super-close friendship, like soul-mates, that somehow our two minds working together could really generate ideas and energy to help the human race. (True, I feel that with Gloria too.) But in Rob's case, I'm kind of afraid he will expect too much of me, that he may have marked me as the person who's supposed to make his life complete. It sounds silly, I know, but I just couldn't handle it if he approached me in a heavy, needy way.

Anyway, Rob and I had a great afternoon, getting stoned and rapping about Castananda and Alan Watts and lots of things. It looks as if he also has definitely decided to go to

UCSC next fall. I like the idea of going off 3,000 miles to college knowing I'll already have a friend there.

Oh, another thought. I definitely like Rob's size. He's tall and solid. Apparently he doesn't waste much time worrying about his body. I like Mark's thinness, but there's a rock-like sturdiness about Rob that I like too. There's a part of me who wouldn't mind being hugged by a big, friendly guy.

Our talk got around to fighting. "I've already decided I'm a pacifist," Rob announced. "I avoid all fights."

"I more or less have, too. But, I don't know. I think I can handle the high school peer-pressure about fighting, but I still wonder whether I might find myself in a situation in which I had to fight either to survive or protect my dignity as a man. Dad was unfairly critical of me when Tom and Joe tried to drag me into that skirmish, but I don't think he realized the bind I was in."

"I see your point but, if you must know, I have little sympathy hearing you complain about your father. It's *my* father who's the Madison Avenue clone. Anyway, I used to get hassled all the time about being a "sissy" since I was so big and it seemed like I was the type that *should* go out for football. That's why your comment at the Cape hurt so much. Now that I insist on being nonviolent, philosophically, no one hassles me anymore."

"Well, the *Lazy Man's Guide* would say you changed your vibrations. Your positive vibes became your protection."

"This is true—at least I hope it is."

"Now that I think of it, Rob, I can think of at least six other nice guys in my class who have never been in a fight either. Who knows, though? My guilty white liberal side says I don't know what I'm talking about—what if we lived in a ghetto?"

"What if? 'What if.' Just try out this theory and tell me if it works," Rob persisted.

"All right. I mean I already am."

Friday, November 17, 1989

Everything's going well with Gloria, when I get to see her, that is. Last night was great. We had the place to ourselves, so I made tacos for dinner. She brought over a bottle of great white wine, and Sally had baked us an apple pie. Afterwards, we just lay around in my room, playing music and being really nice to each other. I guess she has a point. We do seem to appreciate each other more when we see less of each other.

"You know, Gloria, I love the way you twist your hair around your fingers. It reminds me of the neat way Mark sweeps his hair back with his fingers." I paused and grinned, having established deep eye contact. "It also reminds me how you twist me around your little finger, so to speak."

"Stop trying to make me feel guilty. C'mon now. I know you've had good times with Mark and Rob lately."

"Gloria, what I don't understand about you is why you're always so encouraging about my relationship with Mark. I mean I'm jealous a lot—of Becky's closeness to Dad, even of that Donnie-come-lately you dated. Why not you? Are you perfect or something?"

"Lookee here, lover-boy. You do not give me enough space to be jealous. I figure Mark can only benefit from seeing more of you." Sure enough, Gloria started twisting her hair around her fingers. "As for the sexual stuff, well, I am just not threatened. I mean it's not like you have *ever* run out of sexual energy when I've been around. So why worry? Then, too, I think it's important for people to get close to members of their own gender."

"Speaking of sexual energy, I do have rubbers for tonight, although I'm still open to limiting us to just 'safe' sex."

"I appreciate that, Casey. Actually, I do have my diaphragm if we want to use it. I think we might."

We ended up having a great night together. I think our whole style of love-making is changing. Sure we had intercourse for a while, but it was just part of a whole PANOPLY of wonders. (I've been studying vocabulary lists for the College Boards: PANOPLY—PARSIMONIOUS—PELLUCID. Those are typical college board words if there ever were any.)

I love Gloria so much; it's as if she *knows* that everyone is going to like her, that we mortals will always be fighting to try to be with her more. She has a kind of cocky self-assurance, but somehow she still doesn't let her popularity go to her head. Instead, that popularity feeds her determination to pursue a career in medicine and to be her own person. The whole world, sigh, is going to be competing for her love and attention for a long time to come. I may as well accept it.

Monday, November 20, 1989

School is okay, except for Dr. Pompious. The other day he sent me to the principal's office just for dozing off a little in class, and I got detention again. Then he changed my seat to the front of the class, so he could watch me more closely. I ended up next to Mark so we both were kicked out and got detention when we scratched our nails on the blackboard during a boring movie about participles.

Yesterday, he gave us back the compositions we had to do on his topic, *The Value of Friendship*. I put a lot of myself into it and even wrote something about Gloria, Mark, and Rob. He gave me a "D"—a "D"! My first one ever. His only comment was that I deserved to fail because I had written "narrative," not proper "expository prose."

Just as I was trying to figure out how to get revenge on him, this girl, Pamela, who I know is into speed sometimes, suddenly jumped up from her desk, all hysterical, and started yelling at him, "You're a faggot!" Dr. Pompious didn't know what to say or do—so she ranted on, being totally abusive for about five minutes, until Mark and I each grabbed her by an elbow and tried to drag her out of the class. Somebody must have heard her screaming and called the office, because the assistant principal entered, grateful for our help, since she obviously couldn't physically manage Pam by herself. Afterwards, I heard they suspended her for a week and insisted she get professional counseling.

Is Dr. Pompious gay?

Is that why he's so uptight? He's not married, but he flirts with the girls. But it's his own business, anyway. Pam is really playing with fire, causing that kind of a scene in public. Most of the kids just sat there with a smirk on their faces. Maybe he somewhat deserved it, but I still felt kind of sorry for the guy.

Otherwise, things are well. Since I've decided on UCSC, there's no pressure; I've got an excellent record, and they need students. I'm looking forward to college, where you don't sit in class staring out the window while stuff gets explained for the third time.

I've been hanging out a lot with Mark, and I'm glad to be spending Saturdays in the city with Rob. Skiing starts soon, too. And California in a week with Mom for Thanksgiving. Maybe we'll get some sunny, mild weather out there and even hit the beaches.

Saturday, November 26, 1989, Mill Valley, CA.

It's Saturday night of Thanksgiving weekend. Becky and I are here for a week with Mom, Herb, and Danny. We're getting to use one of their cars, so we've taken off for San Francisco and Sonoma County, besides having Thanksgiving here on Thursday. Next year it's Christmas in California and Thanksgiving in Hastings, although now that I'm going to go to college out here, that rotating stuff is just about irrelevant. We've all agreed that from the age of eighteen on, Becky and I can make our own decisions about when to see both Chuck and Diane. I'm grateful that Mom and Dad haven't been at all competitive over the years about seeing us. I know that after next year, when I'm on my own, I'll go on seeing both of them as much as possible.

I need to mention that Thanksgiving was only so-so. Apparently Herb occasionally goes a little wild in his wine cellar and then gets a little outrageous. We handled his celebrating the holiday okay—he was mainly being loud, bragging a lot and trying to shock us with terrible dirty jokes. But his mood caused a regression in my Mom. She began to argue with him, then became almost hysterical. We all really winced when she started bawling and saying stuff like, "What am I going to do if *this* marriage ever fails?"

I tried to be reassuring, but eventually Becky did the most good by gently leading her to her bedroom, talking encouragingly to her for a while and then getting her to take a sedative.

"Holidays," said Danny, up in his room just after things had quieted down, "They are the worst. Most of the time they're both great people to be around."

I was feeling secretly relieved that I had spent most of my childhood with Chuck and Sally. Mom's sort of blowing it had somehow gotten me very upset. "Hey, Casey, don't worry about it. They'll both be fine in the morning. I just happen to have a few lines of coke, especially stashed away to soothe over such emergencies. How about it?"

I told him I'd promised Chuck not to even try coke before I graduated from high school. So we compromised on a drive to San Francisco, just to get out of the house. We found a parking place, smoked a joint, and then took a walk down Polk Street, which, late at night, is a gay cruising area, but which the rest of the time is a hang-out for lots of kids our age who are into the punk scene.

We got high and strolled down toward where most of the action was. While I waited for a red light, I just started talking to this guy named Gary. We had never gotten to dessert at Diane and Herb's, so Danny and I invited him to join us at this great ice cream place. It turns out he's from the midwest, ran away from his family at sixteen. He asked us if we were into men and we said no. He said he wasn't either, but that he sometimes had sex with men to support himself.

I studied him a bit and could see why he might be appealing to a lot of guys. He was sort of tough-looking, sort of good-looking, but still more or less a kid in some ways. I also wondered whether he wanted to have sex with me, but the subject never came up.

"Hey, man, aren't you worried about AIDS?" Danny couldn't help asking him.

"I'm really careful. I know how to play it safe. If someone doesn't like it, he can just take off." Gary's voice was assertive, but his sad eyes suggested that his life-style was more a matter of survival than choice.

I felt sorry for him, being cut off from his family and having to support himself through street life. He seemed really nice, though. (Pat told me most hustlers become cynical pretty quickly.) I told him I was going to college out here and he said he was thinking about school too. I encouraged him, figuring he had plenty of time to turn his life around if he really wanted to. God, I wonder what would life be like if your parents were your enemies? And then I felt so thankful for my family. Mom's hysterics and Chuck's compulsiveness seemed so trivial in comparison.

And then I got this strange feeling as we walked down Polk Street later on. A few of the men were eyeing us in a way that made me feel awkward and self-conscious. If they were attracted to me, it wasn't in a way that made me feel good about myself. Yes, Gloria, it *is* crummy the way men ogle women, too.

The next day Diane and Herb were both apologetic, but really friendly. At about noon we all left for an incredible little trip to Petaluma and Sebastopol up in Sonoma County. Danny told me I'd get "stoked" on the fall colors there after I mentioned being very aware of the autumn back east last month, since it'd be my last one there for a long time. "You won't believe it, Casey. The fall is just starting here. There's still a lot of great color at Christmas."

So we drove up the freeway, exited at Petaluma, and parked on a street with a lot of huge, beautiful Victorian homes. "They were all built with profits from bootlegging," Danny mentioned, obviously regarding his piece of information as quite amusing. Then we walked around for a while. Wow! Beautiful liquidambar trees everywhere, some scarlet, some burgundy. They take three months to change colors and finally lose their leaves in January. And persimmon trees which had lost all their leaves, so that nothing but the bright orange fruit remains. And huge oak trees that were practically blood-red!

Later on, as we drove up Route 116 to Sebastopol and Forestville, I saw lots of apple trees turning color. And golden poplars. And the vineyards—some still greenish-yellow, others burgundy. The east was more spectacular—those red maple trees and red dogwood leaves and berries in our yard! But here the fall lasts so long, if, as Danny keeps saying, "you know where to look for it."

Friday, December 8, 1989, Hastings-on-Hudson, N.Y.

Just when I started feeling everything might flow along well all year, I collided with a terrible downer period. I've been sick, in a bad mood, and arguing with practically everyone. That's par for the course with Becky, but Dad and I are going beyond heated discussions to something more like altercations. I'm even arguing with Sally. Dad says maybe it's the pressure of taking so many tests for scholarships and awards. Maybe I fooled myself into thinking there was no more pressure once I made it into the college of my choice. I know I've had some scary nightmares in which I've forgotten stuff on final exams or haven't shown up for an important test or just plain *failed*.

I still have a couple of grudges against Dad. I resent Chuck's dishonesty about Pat. If Dad loved Pat once in the past, it strikes me as just so arbitrary that Chuck now tells Pat something like, "I like you but we can never again be as close as we once were." Or maybe they feel close to each other without sex—can you feel romantic about someone without sexual feelings? Probably a little, I suppose. My question is what happened after that to his sexual feelings for men?

I guess I should simply allow him his old-fashioned, conventional decision, one appropriate to his generation. After all he was on the Board of Education here and wanted to protect his reputation. Grrrr. Frankly, at this moment, I could care less about his reputation.

I'm also back to seeing a lot of Tom and Joe, just hanging out with them. That's not doing me any good. The last couple of Saturdays with Rob have been uptight ones too. I think he wants to get closer, but sometimes his invitations seem to be pushy. He'd better hold back because I'm not ready. I'm already tired of obnoxious gays trying to make deals with me to pick me up for sex—even though it's only happened once or twice.

Friday, December 15, 1989

That bastard. I'm *so* pissed off at him. He's such a fucking hypocrite. I wish he were home now so I could let him have it, but, typically, he's been coming home late every night from the office, and tonight he's not even coming home at all. I'm totally angry at him; I'd even like to belt him a good one.

He's letting me down. He's laying too many of his own trips on me, too. How I wish I could express myself better. I feel so weird; I know I'm not making sense. Maybe I should just get drunk.

I'm just spinning my wheels. Gloria's gone to a conference of high school editors in Washington, and I know that after she comes back in a couple of days, she's going to be really busy until at least Christmas. I myself just don't feel like doing anything, not even hanging around with Tom and Joe—I'm sick of their stupid stuff too. And I'm tired of Mark's drinking and wild sprees. Somehow, it's better just to stay in my room with all these heavy feelings while I swear and kick stuff around my room. I have so much bitterness to vent towards that defender of human rights; that asshole—he's such a fake. He must be the most confusing person possible to have for a father. I just wish I were out of his home and off by myself. Then maybe I could clear up some of these issues that are eating me up, conflicts caused by the mixed-up messages he's inflicted on me all my life.

Saturday, December 16, 1989

Right now, I am so lonely. I absolutely do not want to meditate or work on mind-training. It is Gloria whom I want, and I haven't met anyone else around here who can even compare. But she is not there when I need her.

Christmas—I could sure do without it. I remember Pat's warning that the Christmas holidays coincide with the time in America when parental expectations hit the hardest. You rate yourself on how well you fit into the mold of exactly what your parents want you to be.

How does that apply to *me*? What am *I* supposed to be? I mean they say anything's okay with them. Why this resentment? Is it what all the psychologists say, that I'm pissed at Dad for being too permissive, for not telling me what to do so I could at least rebel against it? Bullshit! Dad's a little screwed up, but I known he hasn't fucked up my head like most other parents.

I think he's sold himself out to his career. He's less compulsive about being macho than other men, but he's basically driven just like all the other great "successes" in this society. Shit—that's one of the reasons I'm angry—because I don't know what to do. I mean you'd think with these educated parents I'd at least have some focus. Am I ambitious? Sally says I am but don't realize it. But getting into your ambition means driving yourself to success which means becoming a workaholic and not having fun, maybe being sort of happy with your wife and kids, but not being *really* happy.

Sunday, December 17, 1989

You know, I think I *would* like to read Pat's journal sometime to find out what went on in their heads back in college, that is if he's been honest enough to write it down.

How can I be positive during these bummer days? I'm avoiding Sally because I can't stand her sympathy, her condescending attitude that youth must have its pain and suffering. Besides she's been cranky lately too.

Maybe I need to cry. It's so hard to let go; there's no example to follow. That's why I'm so pissed, I think, especially at Christmastime when it seems like I should be measuring up to some standard. Pat's not a good model to follow because he's not bisexual; he's told me about some experiences with women, but he says it's tough for him to be sexually close to a woman. Dad's definitely not the model; I'm pretty sure now that's why I'm so angry, so bitter, why I feel he's let me down so badly.

So, it's up to me. I can do what I want. Right now, I just want to lash out against that crumb for letting me down.

I think I'll write Mom about this stuff; after all, she's a therapist. Hell, there's nothing to lose.

Saturday, December 23, 1989

December 19, 1989
Mill Valley, CA. 94928

Dear Casey,

First, let me tell you how much we loved having you kids for Thanksgiving. Forgive me for letting my past come back to haunt me. I'm determined that it won't happen again. In any case, I'm truly happy you decided to come out here to college. You'll be a couple hours away, enough to ensure your freedom, but close enough for you to spend any free time here you wish. I can't believe you're going to be eighteen in less than a year and that Becky's soon to be "sweet sixteen."

Now let me try to answer some of your questions about Chuck. I don't pretend to be any kind of an expert on this stuff; I'd also prefer to avoid talking about it. But, Casey dear, I want you to know that I deeply sympathize. It's very hard to be a man these days and growing up seems tougher than ever, although maybe some of the reasons for the difficulties have changed. You really need to keep in mind that every son needs to rebel against his father at some time or other and to question deeply the father's value system. There's always some father-son hostility.

I can also see legitimate reasons for your anger. But I can't stop myself from comparing Chuck with other men (including Herb) in his age group and conclude how lucky you kids are. I know his sensitivity and tact during my period of crisis were a great help. He constantly supported my desire to begin a whole new life out here, even though I was so utterly impossible for a while. After all my victimizing, I dare say he wasn't too sorry to have me out of his life.

Well, I should focus my comments on your own conflicts with him. Perhaps the best perspective I can give you on what you're going through (and it seems you are going through an important transition right now) is that you are on the brink of becoming the "new man" that many women think this society needs. That isn't easy because when you're in the front ranks there is no one who's going to reinforce you for being really different, not just in a modish or superficial sense, but really different.

You are approaching the whole matter with much more depth, much more integrity than other men have. I know Chuck's given you mixed messages through the example of his own life, but he can't show you the whole truth—you wouldn't want him to. You know there's a popular expression out here, "Redneck parents have hippie kids and hippie parents have redneck kids." Well it's not always true, but kids do like to upset the parental value system as part of the process of finding themselves.

It's getting tougher to be your own person today, Casey, but you can and will do it, whatever choices you make. Frankly I find it a cause for joyous celebration that my own son is willing to take conscious responsibility for such choices. As much as I love Danny, he's much more typical in that he's kind of falling into his adult identity rather unthinkingly, but then Herb is a much more traditional father than Chuck. Who knows—maybe Danny will learn more about his own inner nature because of knowing you.

That's something that might motivate you onward, the knowledge that without speaking a single word, you may become through your very presence a model for other young men.

Chuck's given you so much, but all human beings are somewhat destructive. Right now, you're wrestling with that element in yourself. There will be many of these symbolic battles, this time it's about relating to men, next time it'll be about something else in all likelihood. I know you'll flow well with everything, my dear son. Spread my love among the whole family.

Much love,
Mom

That letter helps. I feel somewhat better today, although I'm still confused. Mom's right that everything has worked out well so far, so I'm just going to keep flowing along, making decisions moment to moment. It's great that Mom reinforced me for following my intuition.

Finally I'm on vacation. I barely made it. But luckily we don't have to go back until the eighth!

worked out well so far, so I'm just going to keep flowing along, making decisions moment to moment. It's great that Mom reinforced me for following my intuition.

Finally I'm on vacation. I barely made it. But luckily we don't have to go back until the eighth!

PART III

HASTINGS-ON-HUDSON, 1990

Wednesday, January 3, 1990, Hastings-on-Hudson, N.Y.

A perfect winter morning. Went to sleep with snow gently falling. Woke up with the blue spruce almost completely white. Deep snow outside, sheltered and cozy inside, with Buzz snuggled up against my stomach. A new decade! I'm hoping that the nineties will usher in a long period of uncomplicated happiness.

It's been a while since I've written in this, but I've been so busy with the holidays—buying presents, doing chores, seeing people, and going to parties. Besides, before this morning's snow, I was feeling slightly depressed. For one thing, no big surprise I suppose, I've only had a couple of evenings with Gloria this whole holiday season. I've seen a bit more of Dad during the last few days, and we've managed cordial relations, especially on Christmas itself, but I'm still annoyed at him and have generally avoided being alone with him.

Becky's been less of a pain lately since she's started dating Donnie Wilkins regularly about a month ago. At least it keeps her out of the house so she can't dominate the media with all that classical stuff. (I wonder if Gloria passed on any tips to her about Donnie.)

My opinion of Becky is changing fast—for the better. I wonder how close to being a genius she is—you have to be a genius to be a good conductor. I mean, she's still leading the life of a pretty typical teen-ager. Does she have the talent? Does she have the drive to completely devote herself to music? Well, she could become an instrumentalist or a music teacher if she's not a genius.

Sally's been great the whole time. I confess I've been lapping up her sympathy, although I'm still confused about her attitude about the tragedy of adolescence. And with Pat and Eddie around here for a couple of days, it's almost impossible not to have some fun.

I've really been blown away by the changes in Pat since 1982, when he met Eddie. He's so much happier, so much lighter and funnier. He used to be more militant about gay causes, but now he seems to have a good word to say about almost everyone, even ultra-conservatives. Dad told me that Pat used to get very lonely and depressed because he felt so full of love and couldn't find another guy to share that love with.

You can also tell Pat is pretty unthreatened by whatever Eddie does, although he says it wasn't always that way. I really like Eddie too. I hope we become better friends. I still associate Pat somewhat unfairly with Dad's values, but I don't get that feeling from Eddie. Eddie loves to have fun and pull off stunts. I think I might be attracted to him, actually.

Friday, January 5, 1990

DINNER WITH THE STINES

Casey took the disintegrating commuter train into New York City and met Rob at his parents' very elegant East Side apartment about noon. They had a good day seeing a movie, visiting the Guggenheim, and walking about a great deal in the gloomy drizzle. This will probably be my last cold winter for a while, Casey smiled to himself.

The big adventure of the day, however, was having dinner with Rob's folks. Their beautiful apartment in the East Seventies with its expensive furniture and abundance of scholarly books and classical records somewhat intimidated Casey at first. Rob's parents, who dressed rather formally, insisted on being full-time hosts, engaging Casey with questions about Hastings, high school activities, college, his career prospects, his girl friend, and various other topics. Their manner caused Casey to become a bit nervous and uneasy.

He felt a bit more comfortable with Mr. Stine when that distinguished looking gentleman shed his suit jacket, vest and tie, and opened up his starched white shirt collar after dinner. Mrs. Stine was another matter. She was an attractive, youngish-looking woman in her late forties, but she was tense, on edge. The impeccable taste of her outfit only contributed, in Casey's eyes, to make her seem more angular, an effect that fit in with the somewhat shrill, metallic quality of her voice.

As he looked around the luxurious apartment, Casey saw thousands of dollars spent on furniture and decorations, thousands of dollars his own family had not spent on their own suburban outpost. Mrs. Stine would probably call our place "crudely informal", thought Casey.

As the conversation grew dull and both the Stines took advantage of their entrapped audience to elaborate their views on city, state, nation and world, Casey longed to be back in Hastings with Rob where they would now simply go down to the rec room or up to his own room, kick off their running shoes and relax.

Here, tensions were everywhere, in the very air they were breathing. The most obvious ones were between Mrs. Stine and Rob. At times, it seemed as if Rob's hostility would erupt into open warfare with her, and Casey would not have blamed him a bit if it did. She needled, she prodded, she judged, and yet she also seemed desperate for Rob's attention and approval.

Things weren't much better between Rob and his Dad, although Mr. Stine was less domineering and critical, at least on the surface. Casey was surprised that the elder Stine checked Rob out so closely on particular projects Rob was doing for school. Casey's folks trusted him about schoolwork and only talked about it when Casey brought up the subject. They *trusted* him to do well. Wasn't it obvious to Rob's parents that Rob was extremely intelligent and would do well on his own?

"Casey," intoned Mrs. Stine. "I hear from Rob that your father went to Harvard and your mother to Radcliffe! Aren't you going to follow in their footsteps?"

"Actually, I'm looking forward to going to college in California." Casey could sense what was coming—he decided to stay calm no matter how outrageous Mrs. Stine's ploy to discredit UCSC and keep Rob in the east.

"Oh, really." Such a look of disappointment on her face, poor lady! "Recently, Harold and I read about how education in California has gone downhill quite drastically over the last twenty years or so. They used to take such pride in their new universities." She uttered the word "new" as if it were a synonym for "inferior."

"Now, now Julia. Things can't be all that bad out there. Maybe the change will be good for Rob," said Mr. Stine, revealing a surprisingly sympathetic point of view.

Casey looked over at Rob who was in the middle of heaving a huge sigh of relief. He returned Casey's glance with a look of joy. Was this the first time Mr. Stine had given his son such a clear-cut permission to fly the coop?

Casey watched the Stines, fascinated, for a few minutes, as the Stines revealed their relationship in the course of their conversation—the little put-downs by Mrs. Stine, the diminishing, condescending way in which Mr. Stine brushed aside her opinions.

Casey could have used a drink, but none was offered, even though the Stines sipped on their own cocktails before dinner. He guessed Rob and he were considered too young to join them, since Mrs. Stine had only offered soft drinks before dinner and ice tea afterwards. But Rob was on Casey's wave-length, for when Casey excused himself to go to the john, Rob, obviously also needing an excuse to leave the formal dining area, followed Casey out to Rob's bedroom where they smoked a couple of hits and blew the telltale smoke out into the cold, clammy night air. He knew marijuana was out of the question in this household, although he wondered whether the Stine's connected Rob's longish hair and informal clothes with indulgence with this "terrible" drug.

As they returned from this briefest of pitstops with a somewhat more detached perspective, Casey could sense how Rob had loosened up. More relaxed now, they sat back and observed the Stines rave on. No longer did Casey judge. He just enjoyed it all as if it were dialogue in a "B" movie. Their onslaught against Rob continued, each new phase preceded by an innocent-sounding question to Casey. But then they'd switch to Rob as their target, artfully trying to bait him into defending himself.

Soon the not too subtle questions about girls began. Rob had told Casey that his parents had given him a hard time about his not introducing them to any girlfriends. In this exchange, Rob didn't actually say he had any, but he couched his answers in such a way as to invite them to hold on to their illusions.

The whole evening made Casey feel so grateful for all four of his parents. He thought Rob had handled the Stines well, but what a relief to go down to Greenwich Village for expresso after that claustrophobic environment.

The Village was perfect for Casey that evening because he still didn't want to be alone with Rob. Rob said he had been lonely over the holidays and did seem somewhat demanding. Since the Jung seminar was over and they had no plans to see each other for a while, they tentatively decided on a trip to the Cape in April or May.

Saturday, January 8, 1990

With Gloria gone for the final weekend of vacation, I just wasn't going to stay home and have a quiet evening by myself. So I got together with—who else but Tom and Joe. They came over here this afternoon and we drank beer for a while. They mentioned maybe learning some trade after graduation to become an electrician or contractor or something while staying in Hastings. I told them I thought they were nuts, that there was a whole world out there to explore. They just shrugged and Tom kind of glared at me and said, "That's fine for you. But what are we going to do for money. You know my old man isn't loaded like yours."

I wanted to say, "He's not really that loaded," but I checked myself and said instead, "Well, as long as you don't get into a rut. I mean I mentioned it because it's important to have happy lives. It might become deadly dull around here."

Joe cut it off there with a, "We'll see." After a short, awkward silence, Joe mumbled, "Do you two want to go out and do something tonight?"

We all jumped into Joe's car and started talking basketball, especially how our own team was going to improve once the league games resumed after vacation. We were headed down the West Side Drive for Manhattan with no particular plans. Joe, who has been incredibly nice to me since the time we almost got busted, suddenly burst out, "The Knicks. Hey, let's see the Knicks play the Bucks tonight. They finally have a winning record this year, but they're still not selling out. We could pick up tickets there." We all checked our cash supply and decided to be typical fans for an evening.

The Knicks won the game, but it wasn't as much fun as actually playing together. Afterwards we had some wine at a place in Greenwich Village and got back around 2 a.m. I had the feeling that we had spent a lot of money and hadn't had that much fun, even though there was no problem with either of them wanting to do something stupid or dangerous (although Tom *still* made cracks when any weird-looking men passed by the cafe).

Tonight, I got off by myself to mull things over. I admitted to myself I have been somewhat bored when I've been around those guys lately. I've given up trying to influence them, too. For a while, it was nice having friends from outside the suburban crowd who weren't all going on to college. But now I have to admit to myself that we just don't have that much in common. I feel pretty sure I don't want them as close friends any more. GUILT. They'd probably feel let down and accuse me of being a snob who thought I was too good for them.

But then I flipped through *A Lazy Man's Guide* and came across a section about not being obliged to wait out friends with negative energy. If I sense that they are not going to do anything but bring me down, "Just split. Don't dwell on it. It is in the natural order of things," says the *Guide*.

I like the author's use of the word "natural." You can see that Dad was implying that it was natural that I have a friendship with these guys, but that it was also natural I might outgrow them or not need the kinds of experiences they offered any longer. The crucial idea, according to the *Guide*, is not to feel superior. It is in the natural order of things.

It's so beautiful tonight. The snow on the ground is really crusty. I walked in the field across the street under a full moon, crunch, crunching along where nobody had yet stepped. I'll miss the snow.

So it's as if I'm on the brink of a new phase. Already the world of high school seems behind me, but somehow I still have to make it through one more semester.

Tuesday, January 23, 1990

GLORIA SURVIVES A CRISIS

Casey had no sooner settled into the boring routine of his senior year when he was shocked out of his mental hibernation by Gloria's announcement one evening that after missing a period, she had taken tests which proved positively that she was pregnant.

"How?" Casey mumbled, a question that sounded more naive and ignorant than intended. "I mean we've only had intercourse a few times in the last couple of months and you had your diaphragm in every time. It wasn't me who refused to use rubbers."

"I agree. I did take responsibility—I'm not blaming you. It happened that Sunday morning we decided to sleep in at your place, the weekend your parents were away. We had sex that morning without my reapplying the cream. I just totally spaced it out."

"We both spaced it out. I'm sorry, Gloria. It was my fault too. I've been trying to double check you ever since you complained a few months ago. I really did think it was great that you decided against rubbers."

"I appreciate that, Casey. Hey, I'm handling this okay. Mom's already set up an appointment for an abortion. She's been showing me how to keep the trauma minimal. Boy, do I appreciate having a mother like her. No panic, no guilt trips."

"That's great," said Casey, already shuddering with relief. "When's the day? Where can I go? And I want to pay for it too. It's the least I can do."

"Thanks. I appreciate all that stuff. It's in two days, Thursday, up at a women's clinic in Dobbs Ferry. Mom's coming, but says it'd be great if you want to come too. And you can talk with Mom about the money. I'm sure she'll let you pay for half of it."

The day before, Wednesday, Casey and Gloria got together for a cup of tea over at her place. In twenty-four hours Casey had lost his naiveté about abortions. He had helped create a child, his first, and they were not going to allow that child to come into the world. Casey believed that the spirit of the child would find another set of parents, but he couldn't stop imagining what the actual "dead" fetus would look like. It was probably much tougher for Gloria. He asked her if she were feeling guilty.

"And how! I *am* guilty. But my course in life is set. I do want to be a doctor so I can help many, many people, especially women, especially the thousands of poor, single mothers who develop so many diseases from being stressed out all the time. Hopefully, this abortion will benefit them as well as me."

"That makes total sense to me. We're certainly not ready to get married or even live together with a baby. That's inconceivable."

"This is true. But still the guilt comes. Last night I dreamed I was a peasant woman who, when walking down a country road, came upon a straw basket. I picked it up and there, underneath some blankets, was a dead baby. I'll be glad when this is all over."

That Thursday Casey skipped school and drove the ten minutes to Dobbs Ferry to a smallish, modern clinic in a professional neighborhood. Val spent some time in the doctor's office with Gloria, but Casey just sat in the waiting room until they reappeared.

As they drove home, Casey kept stealing looks at Gloria's face. He was impressed. He could see how emotionally difficult it was for her, the violation it must be to a woman's entire system to suddenly be thrust back into an unpregnant state—that had to be some kind of severe physical shock. But even so, Gloria could still smile. Never did she throw one accusing glance at Casey, but he was still relieved that he had, so far, done as much as he could to cooperate with her on the whole issue of birth control.

Not only was he solaced by that thought, he had also discovered, as a result of their being cooperative in this crisis, that it was Gloria's presence, her lovingness and her warmth, that he really loved. And now, her heroic radiance—she could still smile graciously, still cultivate a healthy detachment as her pale, fatigued body started its healing process. She was, after all, going into medicine as a career. Her scientific curiosity made it easier on everyone around her.

What a woman! Casey, feeling somewhat insignificant and out of his element, melted in awe and deep appreciation.

Val invited him in afterwards. She was being so nice too, and Casey was truly thankful. Val understood about Casey's willingness to cooperate. Thankfully, Casey did not need to experience guilt. Empathy was enough, for somehow, despite being male, Casey could sense what Gloria was going through.

As all three of them reached the porch of Val's house, Gloria pounced on her mailbox and screamed in delight after opening a letter. "Mom, Casey, guess what? I've been offered early acceptance with a full scholarship at Stanford. Casey, we'll only be an hour's drive away from each other after all."

Casey received the news with detached joy. He had been sure Stanford would accept her because she had everything they wanted. But he knew he'd keep feeling twinges of envy, for she was so self-directed, so set on a particular career, while he was confronting these economically depressed times by heading off to college with the aim of obtaining an old-fashioned, well-balanced, liberal education (thank goodness his plan had his parents' blessings!)

Casey was indeed relieved that Gloria would be close to him, just over the coastal range, in fact. But he also felt a sobering chill of reality. For the next four years at least, he'd continue to see her only every now and then. Oh well, he was becoming convinced that this part-time stuff with Gloria was a necessity. In fact, they now seemed to be subtly communicating their desire to stay together permanently more than ever before.

And yet, Gloria might meet all these interesting guys at Stanford. Indeed. Casey—and their relationship—would be tested, but it'd be an interesting, fair test. He, in fact, smiled as they entered the house, about as confident as possible, at least for now, that Gloria wouldn't defect to anyone at Stanford. He'd just let things take their course. Nothing terrible had happened yet.

Several days later, Gloria visited Casey up in his room. Buzz snuggled between them in bed as they sipped herb tea from the cups that Gloria had given him. "Casey, I have some post-mortems to share with you concerning my reaction to the abortion." Gloria uttered this statement with a breezy assertiveness that Casey knew meant, "Watch out. Here comes something heavy." She looked him right in the eye and said, "You know, Casey, this stuff has nothing to do with you personally. It has more to do with the world today, the difficult psychological tensions between all men and women."

"Please do continue," said Casey, with more than a bit of trepidation.

"Well, if the abortion has proved one thing to me, it's my very strong desire not to have my sexuality pressured by male demands. Now, it's not you, remember. You've been great, and yet I am telling you now to be very careful about how you come on, at least for the immediate future. I'm glad I have Mom to talk to; it's hard to share with you the psychic consequences of an abortion, the whole wrenching effect. On a gut level I've developed some resistance to intercourse because I absolutely do not want to become pregnant again before I make that choice; yet when I look at your face and eyes, I feel warmth and love and want to be close to you. It's a process that I—that we—need to go through.

"So we need to take things slowly for a while," Gloria continued. "Don't worry. I won't cut myself off from you. I not only love you, I need you, even when I try to act as if I don't."

And with that Gloria pulled up the blankets over them and gave Casey a very big, long hug. How great it was to feel her body flowing with love. He absorbed every last bit of affection and tried to give her back at least as much, if not more.

Casey's heart swelled with love as he gave Gloria another big hug. They snuggled for a while longer and then finally passed out for the night.

Sunday, January 28, 1990

DOUBLE-DATING

If Casey wondered whether the trauma of the abortion would result in a great disruption in his relationship with Gloria, he was reassured a few nights later when Becky and Donnie Wilkins joined Gloria and him for a weird kind of double-date, or at least it felt weird to Casey, not only because it was the first time he had ever gone out with his sister on a date, so to speak, but also because of Gloria's previous date with Donnie. (Apparently her curiosity had been satisfied, because she never went out with Donnie again and never brought him up as a subject for discussion. Casey certainly wasn't going to bring the subject up either, not as long as she didn't show any further interest.)

Casey felt great that evening to be with all three of them, back to a normalcy he had deeply craved during the time of the abortion. He was even getting off on the obvious mutual attraction between Becky and Donnie. He guessed that every big brother probably gets a little shocked when he realizes his baby sister has sexual desires. Becky had, after all, been talking openly about sex for several years and had been more or less dating since thirteen. Nothing like an abortion to help one feel mature, Casey thought, as he realized he had indeed grown out of the stage Becky was now in.

They all drove off to a good film together, followed by a quick visit at a dull local dance, and then back to the McCoy's. Chuck and Sally were relaxing in the living room, so the four of them grabbed some wine and snacks and headed to the rec room, where they plopped down on the mattresses and pillows that lined the walls of the room.

At first they chatted excitedly about local friends and politics. Donnie and Becky were especially impressed with Gloria's admission to Stanford. Soon, however, they all started feeling very relaxed and the talking pretty much ceased. Then Donnie and Becky started kissing, long, sensual kisses that definitely aroused Casey's hormones. He envied them the early stage of their relationship, although since Becky had also been in close touch with Gloria during the abortion, she could hardly *not* have birth control on her mind. Or maybe she and Donnie already had an understanding. Or maybe they were not yet that far along for such considerations?

In any case, Casey was feeling so great that he hardly begrudged his former, now rather unformidable, rival time with his sister. He had, in fact, come to like this guy during the course of the evening. Donnie was nice, appealing, although not particularly stimulating. Maybe that's what Gloria had had to check out. Donnie sure was charming and good-looking, though, with that easy-going smile and Greek-statue kind of hair style that just seemed perfect for a face like his. "Probably any kind of style would look good on him," Casey had to admit to himself.

Then a shudder went through Casey as Becky opened up Donnie's already half-opened shirt and laid her hand across his chest. If only Gloria would do that to him now. (Maybe he, himself, would even like to try going just that far with Donnie, who probably wouldn't even mind.

Casey couldn't imagine him being uptight about anyone touching him.)

It was becoming apparent with each passing moment that Becky and Donnie were going to act as if Casey and Gloria simply weren't there. Casey found it ironic that these younger adolescents were becoming the self-enclosed couple that Gloria would not allow Casey and herself to become. Giving them a few more wistful glances of longing (was Becky's arm purposefully against Donnie's crotch or was Casey imagining in that dim light?), Casey motioned to Gloria toward the door. Evidently, Donnie was going to stay for some time, so Casey decided that he'd be generous and help provide Becky with some privacy. Their exit went unnoticed.

Up in his room, Gloria was invitingly warm. He knew that she had not been aroused by the other couple as he had been, that she was, emotionally, if not intellectually, still reluctant to pursue sexual interaction, that she was still, in fact, feeling like holding back. Casey felt something like nostalgia about the younger couple, as if they represented another, earlier, phase of his life that he really wasn't quite ready to give up. He then remembered that he officially didn't have to give it up yet, that it was okay with Gloria if he wanted to start something with another woman, with anyone, in fact.

His rediscovery that his sense of independence was still intact somehow freed him from any dissatisfaction with his present life. So once again, Gloria and he hugged for a long time, spicing up the warmth they generated with sweet, light kisses. Casey was aroused just about the whole time, but he wasn't impatient. Having accepted the reality of where Gloria was coming from this particular evening, he simply enjoyed himself. As he started falling asleep holding her, his penis remained very stiff. Gloria then turned over on her back and began to play with his cock. Knowing how to give Casey the long, slow strokes that he loved, Gloria brought him to a climax in a couple of minutes. Casey then once again snuggled against her, and they fell asleep.

Friday, February 2, 1990

Ground Hog Day—no sun, and so a positive sign for an early spring. I've been getting antsy lately, probably because I haven't gone out drinking much and have been hitting the books. I knock school a lot, but it's the Mickey Mouse mentality of the bureaucracy that's worse than the courses and teachers, who are pretty fine, actually. I wouldn't mind being a high school teacher some day if I had a lot of freedom to teach what I wanted. I very much enjoy our "enriched" English and history courses. I even finish most of the assignments ahead of time to avoid the pressure of deadlines.

I ended up doing okay with Dr. Pompious, an "A-" in fact, probably because we finally started communicating. After Pamela freaked out, I went in to see him one day after school to explain to him why she was so upset that particular day, what with the drugs and all. I told him that her mother, an alcoholic, had died about three months ago and that everyone in the family was so relieved about it that the kids didn't get to mourn. Their father split years ago, so the older kids are trying to hold the family together. I told Dr.

Pompious that she had probably needed to hurt someone and just chose him as a victim.

Dr. Pompious seemed relieved, actually smiled at me and said, "Casey, I really appreciate your taking charge when she went out of control. This kind of thing has happened to me before, although never in such an open confrontation. I guess the way I talk and move my hands reminds some people of how they think gay men act. But actually, you know, I'm engaged to be married this June to a very lovely woman, and I'd like your whole family to come to the wedding."

This was back near the end of the semester, with our term projects due for him in a couple of weeks. So he then asked me what mine was about. I told him, and then we sat down and started to put an outline together. He gave me many good suggestions for books and told me he'd throw out my early grades if my project was really good. I did work hard on it, but I also got the idea that he wanted to make up for being so tough on me back in September and October.

So ol' Pompious is "straight" after all—you just can't tell these days. Well, I certainly don't begrudge the old grouch a happy marriage and a lot of good sex.

Speaking of which, I haven't seen Gloria as much as I'd like, as usual. As to starting a second romantic relationship, I figure I'm a "lame duck" in Hastings anyhow, leaving pretty much for good in June. So I'm beating off with some regularity, usually late at night. I have this synthesizer tape that's all Bach—beating off to Bach.

Anyway, last night was different, both scarier and better. I took Pat's suggestion to regard sexual energy as simply one aspect of the life-force. So I decided I'd try to feel some *love* for each woman who appeared in my mind's eye as I jacked off. That felt good. Then I tried to forget the fantasies altogether and just chant to myself "expand in love" as I continued to beat off. That felt *really* good. I did get hit by some guilt that I was being a bit blasphemous, but Pat had warned me that might happen if I tried to mix sex and spirituality. He said our society frowns on any such attempt, so most all of us remain in conflict in our attitudes.

I don't know whether there was any connection with my experimenting last night, but I felt great today. I played lots of pick-up basketball after school and I've been *running* all my errands every chance I get. In the spring, I'm going to join some of the guys from the cross-country team who are organizing an informal club to stay in shape during the off-season.

Tuesday, February 21, 1990

TOO MUCH HOT-DOGGING

Casey and Mark left very early for skiing Saturday, planning to spend two nights near Sugar Loaf at a cabin owned by one of Chuck's friends. They were on the slopes most of Saturday having a good time, but Mark wanted to try more daring runs. Let's face it, thought Casey, he's an excellent skier. God, he pursues it with a fanatical energy. Me, I like it, but this is only my second time this year. I haven't really gotten into gear yet on the slopes. "Why not split up tomorrow?" Mark's face lit up when Casey made the suggestion. The thought of two days by himself on the slopes definitely picked him up.

"Thanks, Casey. I need my hit of thrills. Going fast, zipping through the snow, leaping over jumps, I enjoy that. I love that sense of freedom, of completely getting away from everything else."

"Just be careful, Mark."

"Case-see. I didn't come up here to be careful, big Mama Casey. Let your little boy have some fun."

Of course, they went to the Sugar Loaf Lodge that evening and just hung around, too young to be admitted to the bar, but not to flirt with some of the women. They did get a friendly college guy to buy them a bottle of Bacardi 151-proof dark rum, something they had never tried and had always wanted to. What better time than before a fire on a winter's night in Vermont. They even bought some "hot buttered rum" mix to do it up all proper. (Yum, all those preservatives, thought Casey, defiantly.)

Upon returning to the cabin, they proceeded to get stoned, to drink, and to play some tapes on Mark's equipment. Around eleven, they let the fire run down and immediately jumped into bed since the temperature inside started dropping quickly.

At first, they avoided body contact, turning their backs to each other as if they were going to fall asleep immediately. But the sheets were so cold that it seemed perverse to deny the aid of body heat, especially with a boyhood playmate. Casey's pride broke first and he whined in a silly, halting voice, "Markie, how about of bit of physical proximity to help your old pal, Casey, stay warm?"

Mark replied in a comic militaristic fashion, "Fuck you, faggot. I'm out of that scene with you." But, even as he spoke, Mark slid over sort of next to Casey, unable to resist his friend's appeal to logic, although still with his back turned.

Well, Mark's hyper-thin body no doubt contained less than 0.001% body fat. What good did that do for Casey? You had to have a lot of skin-to-skin, molecule-to-molecule contact with Mark to generate any BTU's. So Casey grabbed Mark rather rudely around the ribs, flipped him over and pushed his own derriere right into Mark's gut. Yes, there's where the warmth was, where Mark's inferno of a metabolism turned thousands of calories a day into high energy.

Maybe it was the dope, maybe it was the booze, but Casey instantly got hard the moment Mark's stomach made contact with his backside. Hell, that guy's aura just feels so good, filled with that high he has all the time—except during those recent periods of depression. So Casey rolled over and lay his face against Mark's face. He was surprised by the sensation from touching Mark's beard, which was more there than usual since Mark hadn't shaved in two or three days. He also felt Mark's moustache. Both whiskers and moustache made him feel tingly.

Then Casey rolled off Mark onto his back. His nose was very close to Mark's armpit. Mark had not showered for at least a day. Sometimes Casey could just barely pick up something resembling that same sweaty smell on Gloria. He liked the suggestion of the odor on her, and he liked Mark's stronger, more pungent smell too. Once again he rolled over, this time spreading one hand over Mark's chest. He discovered that the nipple under his hand was hard. He also discovered a few moments later that Mark's cock was hard.

Almost slurring his words and thereby discovering conclusively that he was very drunk, Casey murmured some sweet nothing like, "Look, Mark, just because we're a bit turned on doesn't mean anything."

Casey had gone too far. Mark was harsh in his reaction. "You bet we don't. Hands off. I'm through with that stuff. Let's go to sleep. I really want to do some wild skiing tomorrow."

Backing off, Casey grabbed onto the blotto-land express with mixed emotions. Really, they should stop this kind of immature situational sex and should decide, as two nearly grown-up people, whether or not they wanted a physical relationship. It occurred to Casey that Mark had been acting lately as if he didn't want any kind of relationship with anyone. He felt a twinge of sadness that he and Mark might be growing apart.

The next day, Sunday, they spent away from each other, each one choosing slopes which challenged him to his limits. Later at dinner at the lodge Mark talked excitedly about the many thrilling runs he had that day. Casey listened good-naturedly. He too had had a good day, trying some new things, sort of glad to experiment away from the curious gaze of Mark's expert eyes. Since they still had half a bottle of that killer rum left, they then resorted to the same pattern as the previous night—a fire, hot-buttered rums, weed, cold sheets, and then what?

Casey knew something was different about Mark tonight. Daredevil skiing had given him an air of self-confidence. As Casey shuddered in the cold sheets, he thought, I love this moment right now no matter how cold I am. At that instant he felt Mark moving towards him. In fact, Mark abruptly burrowed under the covers, crawled on top on Casey and put Casey's cock into his mouth. Caught by surprise, for the briefest of moments Casey adamantly refused to give his cock permission to cooperate, preferring to nurse a hurt from the night before. Once again, demon alcohol came to Casey's rescue. Why the hell not, thought a much stronger, more sensually pragmatic side of himself. In moments, Casey's penis was hard. A couple of minutes later, he swiveled around so that he could suck Mark's cock without interrupting Mark (hardly).

Yes, we're quite drunk again, thought Casey as they took a break from explicit sexual activity to roll around the bed together, entwined in the shape of a very lopsided ball. No words were spoken during the whole episode. Casey hungrily rubbed his own beard against Mark's beard, then against his neck. He got very tingly. They actually hugged a few times too. Finally. What love Casey felt coming from that rubbery body.

Only Gloria could rival that energy. What warmth he felt in Mark's cock as they beat each other off.

After coming almost exactly together, they drifted off to dreamland, Casey snuggling Mark. How lucky to have this guy for a friend, thought Casey, and then they turned over once more and Mark held Casey. When Mark gets past his hang-ups and gives into his good vibes, thought Casey, there is hardly anything like it—except Gloria.

The next day, Monday, Washington's Birthday, they split up again. Casey knew something was wrong when, at the end of the day, Mark didn't show up at the lodge. Instead, after he had waited around for a half hour or so, Casey was approached by one of the staff at the lodge who inquired, "Are you Mark Gardner's friend?"

Casey nodded yes and learned that Mark had been taken to the local hospital. He immediately drove there to discover that Mark had not only broken his leg but that he had a back injury with possible complications. Knowing how devastating any loss of mobility would be to Mark, Casey was stunned.

It happened that Mark was in a silly, spaced mood, no doubt due to sedation and pain-killers. "Casey, you wouldn't believe some of the runs I had. I got way off by myself at one point and actually flew off a cliff, maybe thirty feet high or so; it just came out of nowhere."

"So that's how it happened. You went 'splat' after trying to fly off a cliff."

"No, no," Mark jumped in, "that's the weird part. I landed *perfectly* and began skiing again as if nothing had happened. As I was soaring through the air, the thought occurred to me that there might be an avalanche when I landed on the powder. In fact, the whole slope did start to slide, but I went shooting out to the side and grabbed some trees."

"Well then, tell me, tell me. How did it happen?"

"I guess I let that narrow escape go to my head and started thinking I was superman or something. So I stayed off the regular slopes and tried this really steep drop where there were a lot more trees. I was doing fine, except that, about halfway down, I hit a hidden rock and went flying through the air, head over heels, here's your 'SPLAT', right into a tree. Listen to the birdies sing! I knew I had blown it, being out of bounds and all, but I managed to get my skis off and crawl a few hundred yards back to where I knew someone would be coming by."

Mark seemed to be caught up in telling and retelling his disaster. It occured to Casey that he seemed like a young war hero bragging about his battle ribbons. Something annoyed him about Mark's attitude. First of all, Casey couldn't help matching himself against Mark's reckless style and feeling something less than a man. But another side of Casey thought Mark foolish, stupid even; he could almost picture Gloria's disgusted reaction. Yet, as Sally would, he felt an urge to console Mark for being so badly hurt and also wanted to somehow convince him to give up his wild, destructive side, once and for all. A part of him even felt relieved that he was moving away from Mark, because he didn't want any more destructive friends like Tom and Joe. And then, Casey was jolted into the awareness that Mark's self-destructiveness might have been caused by his guilt about the affectionate sex they had had the night before. Can he be that messed up, thought Casey? I can't believe it's that big a deal to him.

Casey called Chuck and got permission to miss school to stay another day with Mark. On Tuesday they put the cast on Mark's leg, declared a clean break and said his back seemed okay after all. It was a slow, dull day, as Mark dozed through most of it. Casey read one of his assigned texts, so he wouldn't fall behind at school. He left about three so that he'd drive most of the way home during daylight. As he drove through the wintry, barren woods, he felt sorry that Mark had to lie around that dreary little hospital watching TV for several days and then spend six weeks in the cast. Already Casey planned to volunteer to drive up with Gloria on Thursday to pick Mark up, since the doctor in charge decided it was better to release someone as energetic as Mark as soon as possible.

Saturday, February 24, 1990

LIFE WITH GLORIA

Gloria did make the trip up with Casey. Initially, she was not in a good mood. Once out of Westchester, she indicated that she needed to talk again about the sexual side of their relationship. "Casey," she began, "I just will not have you pressuring me any more."

"What pressure? I haven't tried to force anything on you."

"There's indirect pressure too, you know."

"What do you mean?" Casey winced as he waited for specifics.

"Remember when we were up in your room about a month ago. I was all ready to fall asleep, but you were so aroused. I felt sympathy for you and wanted you to have an orgasm to ease your frustration. But afterwards I didn't feel so good about it. It was as if I had given in to pressure from you, as if I had 'serviced' you."

"Gloria, are you trying to make me go nuts? I took that as a gift from you. Just because I have a hard-on doesn't mean I have to have a climax. I thought we were clear on that. I felt no need of climax at all that night. If you want, I can try to censor my erections when you're not in the mood."

"Don't be sarcastic. I don't want to go on about this, you know. It's just that I had a negative reaction afterwards. You mean you *really* didn't expect anything then?"

"Of course not. I was almost asleep."

Gloria seemed confused, frustrated. Tears started down her cheeks. Casey was surprised to see her out of control.

"I don't know, Casey. Maybe I'm just upset by Mark's accident. I worry about his thrill-seeking not so much because I think he's going to do himself in. No, I worry because physical challenges seem to be the only way he gets any self-esteem. Sometimes I think he's intimidated because he's surrounded by so many smart, verbal females that maybe he feels intellectually and emotionally inferior."

"I think you're right, Gloria. I guess he just needs some time away from our families. Maybe he could travel on his own after graduating, working on a ship or as part of some kind of exchange program."

"Not a bad idea. But let's not mention it to him for a while. With Mark, you have to select your moments carefully."

"I know, I know," said Casey with mock-heavy irony, remembering his two very different nights in the cabin with Mark on their skiing weekend. And then his face brightened at the realization that he'd be staying in the same cabin tonight, this time with Gloria. Trying to stifle his expectations, Casey couldn't suppress a hope, a hope that in this super-romantic setting Gloria would be ON tonight, full of love and sensual energy as only she could be. The odds were good. He hadn't seen her for several days, and the situation with Mark had pulled them closer together as teammates, fellow Mark-rescuers.

When they arrived at the hospital, Mark was in good spirits, happy to see them both and eager to leave. One of the nurses indicated that she thought Mark had recovered remarkably quickly. That usual glow surrounding Mark would heal anyone, thought Casey. They hung around with him until about nine at night, the end of visiting hours. Then they left, telling him they'd be back to pick him up at ten the next morning.

They drove slowly back to the cabin, where they savored the amenities: wine, snacks, and the fire. Casey felt great; he was totally happy to be in this place with Gloria, knowing that he was going to enjoy every minute of it. He figured his euphoric state was a legacy from Mark, for if Mark were radiating towards health so quickly, some of that energy had no doubt rubbed off.

"You know, Gloria, I think there's something really great in the air when you and Mark are together and are both feeling good. In fact, I will admit I sometimes get a bit turned on to Mark when I see the ways in which he resembles you."

"That's sweet Casey-cakes, but maybe you ought to try admitting to yourself that you're turned on to Mark—period. I can't say as I blame you. Sometimes I think I'm almost attracted to him too. Imagine, tackling the terribly heavy taboo of INCEST! Seriously, though, how can you resist him Casey: that smooth, downy-soft skin, that long, stretchy, energy-charged body, that puppy-cute boy-face"?

"Yeah, that's the way all you women are, looking at men as nothing but sex objects." Casey paused, waiting to enjoy Gloria's sarcastic smile. "Actually, though, aren't women more attracted to the overall vibes of a man? Your minds don't obsess the same way as men's about sexual objects—or do you hide much of your raw, physical desire?" Casey finished his question with an attempt at a lecherous smile.

"Of course we hide it. We're told a million times to hide it. But I think you're right, generally speaking. We look for an overall personality with which we can flow comfortably. That's what I really mean by Mark's being attractive to me. When I got over the adolescent blues at about fifteen, I looked at Mark and said, 'That brother of mine is one high person. Why can't I be as consistently happy as that?' "

"Exactly. But lately he's not been so happy, don't you think?"

"He's not being honest with himself. He's not interested in dating now, not even pretending to be. So if he's not interested in women, he's probably interested in men. But he's not admitting it. He's compensating by becoming more macho, more hooked on overcoming challenges."

"I don't know, Gloria. Mark's a funny guy. Maybe he just needs to be independent of *everybody* for a while."

"You see, Casey, you have a big advantage; you've already developed a side of you that can relate emotionally and sexually to women. You can take or leave men." Gloria paused for a few seconds. "In any case I guess it wouldn't come as any great shock to you if I told you that I myself am now open to the possibility of a close relationship with a woman."

Casey was struck silent for a few moments. He gulped, then tried to recover with, "Of course not. I mean I'm sure I'd be *somewhat* threatened. So that's why you've given me so much freedom to open myself up to a close relationship with another guy. Well, I'm not sure I want that freedom." But Casey did think to himself that the freedom was there if he needed it.

His mind switched quickly back to Gloria's statement about her loving women.

"Er, uh, Gloria, do you have anyone specific in mind?"

"Well, I was thinking of Rob. When I met him..."

"Gloria! For crying out loud, I meant for you, not for me."

"Well, there are a couple of friends in Boston, but I can't tell you any details yet. Maybe I'll work out a summer fling with one of them before departing for wild, sick California!"

"It's okay with me. But I sort of envy you women. It seems more acceptable today, at least in reasonably civilized circles, for a woman to get together with another woman. I definitely feel I'm fighting my own inner stigma about guys. Since I have a girlfriend, I figure why risk so many consequences just to have sex with a guy?"

"The stigma is in your head, although I agree with what you just said because I'm scared of being closer to women myself. I'm not ready yet, although I sometimes have dreams about it. And, being afraid, I close off to women. Then I become immediately jealous of you and your men friends. I'm even a little bit threatened by someone as attractive and intelligent as Rob. I say to myself, 'If Casey gets over his hang-ups about men, he might become closer to Rob than he is to me.' "

"Gloria, I can't believe my ears. Evidence of some insecurity. You're human after all."

"Yes, but I've also discovered I can accept *your* bisexuality more easily than my own. Believe it or not there's a part of me that would like to be a 'straight' housewife with a successful husband and a bunch of kids. Maybe that's the way I could best rebel against Val. God, back when I was thirteen I used to fight with her all the time about how she was poisoning my mind. I made life hell for her for a couple of years then."

"I can hardly believe what you're saying. You two have always presented a pretty united front."

"It *was* a front. Well, actually not, I guess. I think I was just testing her, giving her a hard time. She's strong, she could take it, I figured. Finally I realized that she was the kind of woman I wanted to be. And then, a couple of years ago, we did really become friends."

"You mean about the same time you and I became, uh, lovers?"

"That's no coincidence, Casey. You're so mellow there was no way I could be close to you until all that stuff with Mom was somewhat cleared up. Anyway, lover-boy, no need to worry about it tonight. Let's be Mark-in-the-moment with each other tonight. Is that okay with you?"

Needless to say, Gloria was in rare form. The trauma of the abortion was no longer bothering her. Casey started feeling not only happy, but almost solemn. He was very gentle and careful. They did a lot of sensual kissing, hours of it, hugging each other gratefully, time after time. When they were ready for intercourse, he insisted on using a rubber. He kept his penis inside of her for a long time. It stayed hard and felt really good without his having to move it very much at all. A rubber and no movement—it sounds so unsensual and yet they were totally surrounded by all this warmth, all this love which poured out of their beings into each other.

The next day, the three of them had a great trip back, laughing all the way because it was a school day and they all were together. Casey could tell that it was starting to hit Mark that both Gloria and he would be gone the following year. "I'm going to miss all the good times with you two," he even mentioned at one point.

Back home, Casey was still superstitious about coming to positive conclusions about his relationship with Gloria, but he felt that his sexual restraint had increased her trust in him. Shit, it must be so heavy to have to have an abortion, he thought. Casey was particularly grateful that Gloria was so strong, so healthy, both mentally and physically. "Gloria, I think you're just great," Casey shouted out later that evening in his room by himself. "You're one fine woman."

Thursday, March 8, 1990

I let Gloria read some of my practice narratives in this journal for feedback. She replied, "It's a good start, Casey. I love the play of your mind. But, you know, only a few people are into that. You need more concrete description of people, places, and things. You're too into your own mind. Be more dramatic. Show, don't tell, but do keep it up."

She's right, of course, but sometimes I wish she wasn't so direct. (My fragile writer's ego crushes so easily.)

I've been stoked on finding out how good the fall and winter weather is in Santa Cruz, that they even have a big surfing tournament there Thanksgiving weekend. I want new experiences, new friends. I want to go to small seminars where everyone's really interested; I want to be outside, exercising in the warm sun all year, really making use of my time—college, work, and play—the golden mean in the Golden State!

Speaking of school, I hope I find teachers like Pat at UCSC. I've been thinking a lot about Pat lately and about how good an influence he's been on all of us. I'd like to be a lot like him.

What I'm stalling about saying is this—if I enjoy being physically close to guys, why shouldn't I stay in touch with that side of me? I am, however, far from completely accepting this emotionally, although Gloria's insistence on her becoming closer to women has definitely helped me let go of some of my resistance. O Gloria, my teacher, my lover, my friend.

Tuesday, April 10, 1990

SPRING BREAK

Friday afternoon, right after school got out for spring vacation, Casey and Gloria (ecstatically happy to have a week off from school) drove to New York City to visit Rob. Casey looked forward to this weekend for not only were Rob's parents away, but they planned to see a revival of *The Rocky Horror Picture Show* at midnight. Then on Saturday morning they'd all drive up to Boston to drop Gloria off for a weekend with her friends there. Then Rob and he would spend a couple of days on the Cape.

Casey had only been to the Cape once in the spring, many years ago, so he was particularly curious to see what it was like. He did have some apprehension about being alone with Rob for a couple of days. He certainly would have preferred Gloria. But there was no way she was going to be talked out of visiting her mysterious women friends in Boston. Well, then, that being the case, he figured he might as well try to have a really good time with Rob.

Everything went smoothly at Rob's apartment. The doorman was expecting them and parked their car in the Stine's vacated space. Rob greeted them with mock-grandiosity, stiffening his face and talking like a snobby English butler. He then marched them into the kitchen and presented primo ingredients for a huge Mexican dinner. Casey peeked into the refrigerator, as he was wont to do, and saw sixpacks of Dos Equis and Carta Blanca. "Yum. Rob's really prepared," thought Casey. Smoking dope as if it was disappearing the next day from the face of the earth and playing rock music very loudly, they cooked and devoured a hugely satisfying meal. Luckily the neighbors must have been out because there were no angry thumps on floors, walls, or ceiling.

Meanwhile all three of them talked like crazy. Gloria and Rob hit it off especially well that particular evening. They discussed politics, music, psychology, metaphysics; it didn't seem to matter what, both Gloria and Rob had the ability to make sense about everything. Gloria had also enrolled in the seminar on dreams, so they all had a ball trying to remember the weirdest moments in their dreams. Casey played the clown to keep things light and they all laughed a lot at his silly comments, for they had been released from school and now had a week of actual freedom!

At about eleven Rob produced a thai stick of incredible potency, its dosage being such that the simple walk to the movie theatre became an exciting journey through strange buildings, alien faces, and neon lights. Once they reached the line for the show, however, their sense of feeling weird out on Gotham's streets completely dissolved as they settled in for the colorful wait with fellow members of their tribe, many of whom were dressed up in wild, outlandish costumes. "Strange things are happening," Rob intoned. His favorite expression was certainly appropriate to this scene. The time passed quickly as they alternately gaped and chatted.

"I love gender-fuck," said Gloria, as they emerged from the theater afterwards. "Now, let's hope the 90's come up with a whole mess of wild *new* books and movies."

Exhausted by the late hours, the guys mumbled in agreement as they walked quietly home to a good night's sleep.

Later Casey and Gloria got to make love in the Stine's very elegant master bedroom. Rob had urged them to sleep there. "Maybe you two will improve the energy in there if you use it," Rob had reasoned. Casey thought Rob was putting on a brave front in that Casey kept wondering about how Rob felt about being left out. But he also felt extra permission to be sensual and naughty with Gloria, too. He deliberately made sure at least a tiny bit of sperm got on their sheets.

The next morning they had a big breakfast and hit the road, dropping off Gloria in Boston in time to meet her friends for dinner. Casey and Rob immediately drove south to the Cape, arriving on a cold, drizzly evening about eight. Casey quickly rustled up a dinner from various dry goods and cans abandoned the previous summer. It was a trashy dinner, but somehow a fitting complement to the perfect meal of the previous night. Afterwards, to get a bit of exercise, they took a walk around the tiny town. Absolutely nothing was open, of course. They returned, refreshed the fire and finished their quiet evening by reading for an hour or so before going to bed.

Now it was time for the touchy subject of sleeping arrangements. Casey didn't have any objections to sleeping with Rob. They had done so several times on crowded, summer weekends. "How about our using the master bedroom, since it's downstairs and close to the fireplace."

"Sounds fine." Rob immediately tossed his small backpack on the double bed, obviously ready to retire.

Casey was tired from the day's travelling. While Rob brushed his teeth in the adjoining bathroom, Casey jumped into the bed. It was so cold under the sheets Casey had no regrets about lying next to Rob's large body for warmth. But deep down inside he was afraid Rob would "try something." He didn't though. They fell asleep immediately, backsides almost touching, and woke up the following morning in the same position.

It was a clear Sunday morning, but the temperature had jumped up significantly with the disappearance of the damp, clammy fog. Casey *loved* having Granny McCoy's house all to himself, so much so he wasn't even tempted to blow some bucks at a restaurant. Instead, planning to eat dinner in, they set off for a daytime visit to Provincetown. By now the clouds were starting to break up and some undeniably warm sunshine was flooding through the gray. The Cape was still wintry—no leaves on the trees, the forsythia just beginning to form buds, only some crocuses and a very occasional daffodil in a sheltered nook had made it to the blooming stage. (Casey wondered what Northern California looked like that very moment as they zipped by the worst areas of tourism's conquests on Route 28.)

By the time they had made the left turn to drive up the Cape's dramatic northern peninsula, the weather had become completely sunny with only the very softest of breezes. "In good weather, there's so much you can do," said Casey, totally delighted at this sudden turn of meteorological events. "We could go to the sand dunes and lie in the sun—maybe even plunge in for a mini-instant! Or we could stroll around P-town, maybe even go to one of the beaches there."

"Let's do both. Let's go to Wellfleet first, just in case the weather changes later. I think I can really get off on the beach."

"Great," responded Casey. So they climbed down the dunes at Wellfleet to a surprisingly warm beach below, a surprisingly narrow beach too, as the winter storms had taken their toll on the usual summer sandiness. Predictably, they ate some dope crunchies and just melted into the sun, daring it to leave any faint traces of pink on their pasty-white bodies.

After a whole winter of cold, Casey had no trouble in just absorbing every bit of the sun's warmth directly into him. The crunchies soon took effect and he started to float into a trance. Suddenly he experienced a strange sensation. Although Rob was sprawled on his back with his eyes closed about a foot away, Casey was gradually becoming aware that Rob and he were sharing the same mind-space. It felt good, a quiet, wordless sharing.

Yes, thought Casey, this sharing certainly was a sign that at least part of himself trusted Rob. Otherwise he would never open up in this way. Casey wondered for a moment whether he and Rob could develop telepathic communication, but he dropped his musings as he felt the tie with Rob weakening, for it does take some concentrating to maintain a mind-meld.

They never made it to P-town. Instead they explored the beach, walking miles north where they once again lay in warm, naked isolation. They even took a couple of icy plunges, after playing lots of frisbee to build up a sweat. The day passed quickly, for the sun still set early. They just barely made it back up to the highway to watch the sun go down and to see the colors of the afterglow reflected on the calm waters of the inner bay.

Later, back at the house, they kept the same sleeping arrangement as the previous night. This night, however, just before they pulled back the blankets, Rob jumped Casey and gave him a long hug. While it was in progress, it did pop into Casey's mind that he had been relieved that earlier in the day, while skinny dipping and lying in the sun, Rob had shown no signs of being aroused. The hug, too, was only a friendly ritual. They were both asleep minutes afterward.

The next day, Monday, their final one on the Cape, they locked up the house early in the day and drove to the ferry at Buzzard's Bay to go to the Vineyard, for Val's sister, Mark's Aunt Mary, was expecting them. Funny, whereas Casey was so glad Mary couldn't accompany Mark and him on their excursion to discover Leslie and Adrienne last summer, now he was just as glad that she *was* free to spend the afternoon with them, for Casey welcomed a relief from the intensity of being alone with Rob. For all Rob's seeming restraint, Casey still felt a kind of pressure. Sensing this awkwardness in Casey, Rob would then occasionally worsen Casey's self-consciousness by backing away from Casey with typically comic self-parodies whenever they both noticed they were physically close. So it was just as well they all became tourists for the afternoon. All three of them in fact took turns at the wheel as they explored the entire coastline of the Vineyard. It was another beautiful day, although this one was considerably cooler, with a typically stiff, biting sea breeze. Aunt Mary treated them to a coastside lunch of clam chowder and lobster. How beautiful the sea looked as they sat in the warm sun, protected by a glass wind-break at the restaurant.

And then inevitably back to the ferry, then to Boston to pick up Gloria and the long drive to New York City. They dropped off Rob about ten, declining the option of staying over another night.

A day later Casey felt as if the weekend with Rob had been fine, but he was also ready for another breather. Despite their mutual restraint, Casey felt the weekend had significantly deepened their friendship.

Casey wondered whether Rob longed for him the way he had longed for Gloria in that year of dating before they had sex. Was Rob in love with him? Casey decided he was just barely able to handle the situation. He also knew that he needed to talk to Rob about their feelings for each other. But not for a while.

Friday, April 28, 1990

Almost the end of April; that's three week's of not writing in here. I *am* ashamed, although there's not too much to summarize. So far the seminar on dreams has been great, although, unlike Gloria, I seem to be avoiding writing down my dreams, the few I can remember, that is. Still I'm absorbing a lot from the course. Maybe the best part of it is that all three of us, Gloria, Rob and I, get together and bullshit after class. Rob and Gloria are both so sharp; sometimes I fantasize we could all make great collaborators on some kind of new-age project or be part of some kind of new-age community.

Last weekend's seminar was a shocker. This anthropologist, Tobias Schneebaum, visited as a guest lecturer to talk about some of the primitive tribes of Asia. He told us about how the Senoi share their dreams with each other every morning and even let their dreams tell them when to plant or harvest. But the real shock came from his disclosure about the Amsat tribes in New Guinea, at least the ones with whom he lived on the south coast. Apparently every adolescent boy is paired with another male with whom he becomes best friends *and* lovers until one of them dies. Marriage and family life go on as usual, too. I remember that Pat told me the same kind of thing happens in Nepal where every guy has a "dear friend." So there's absolutely no stigma in those cultures. Frankly I was shocked. (I wonder if the "dear friend" and the wife are ever brother and sister.)

Gloria and I are arguing again. She says I don't listen to her when she gives me criticism—usually for being too intense or for putting too much sexual pressure on her. What does she expect? I used to think she was going to work through this stuff and then she'd want to spend all her time with me. But now a nagging sense of realization is hitting me. Things are going to be *always* more or less like this. If I'm in a good mood, a part-time relationship seems like a great idea, but when I'm a little down I wonder how long I can put up with it without becoming a wimp.

And speaking of being a wimp, that's how I feel in gym class lately. We *had to* take a month of wrestling. I never really tried—I just lost. Sometimes my partners knew what I was up to and we'd just go limp together. That really pissed off Coach Powers. For trying to turn his program into a farce, he'd just stand above me most of the period, taunting me all the time about being a sissy. I thought about destroying his career with an A.C.L.U. suit.

I've hardly seen anything of Tom and Joe this semester, except at our league basketball games. (I get the sense they're trying to avoid me lately.)

My favorite teacher, Frank Adams, besides being into American history, is a nature nut who also loves to run. So he agreed with our idea to start a club to meet after school twice a week in order to go out running on beautiful and unusual courses in parks or woods or whatever. The great part is that I got Mark to join as well as Gloria and Becky. That Gloria is such a jock. I'll never be the swimmer she already is; man she really packs a pair of shoulders. Sometimes in bed she pretends to pin me. I'm reluctant to try to fight my way out because I wouldn't be surprised if I couldn't.

Well yesterday both Frank Adams and Becky were sick and Gloria had to spend the afternoon pasting up the next edition of the *Hastings Buzzer*. At first the five of us guys who showed up thought we'd just go home and forget it. But it was such a warm, sunny day and I was up for doing something outside. So I yelled out, "Hey, let's all run up the aqueduct to Tarrytown. We don't need a car for that."

Everyone agreed, especially when Mark added a great twist. "Okay, I'll go, but only if we drink a beer at every town along the way."

"On the way back too?" asked Donnie Wilkins, obviously going for the program.

"But we're not old enough to buy any," I realistically intruded. "Let's settle for a little smoke instead."

Well, we jogged up the aqueduct, a wide, flat trail over the pipe that carried New York City's water supply south through the various towns along the Hudson River. It is high enough to allow beautiful views of both the river at its widest as well as the purple, sheer cliffs of the Palisades on the Jersey side. It cuts through centuries-old grand estates originally settled by the Dutch.

Spring was bursting out and in all the beautiful gardens along the way, everything was lush, the way I love it. You could smell both the pink cherry blossoms and the white apple blossoms. The run to Tarrytown was totally pleasant. We immediately turned around and ran south to a playground in Irvington, dotted with a field of blossoming magnolias. We got high—and suddenly the world was incredibly beautiful.

Semi-zonked crazy man Mark pulled down his sweatpants—he was wearing a jock underneath—and slid down the steep, cold, shiny-surfaced slide on his bare buns. He didn't slide so well either, just kind of bumped his way down, his skin making screeching sounds when in contact with the slide.

Everyone laughed at his failure to re-live his childhood thrills. Then the other guys started messing around too. Derek, who I've always had my suspicions about, grabbed the buns of his friend, Bob, and said comically, "Wow, it's such a great day and I'm so horny that I could almost go for guys."

Bob acted shocked and physically shoved Derek away, spitting on the ground to communicate his apparent disgust at the idea. But that wasn't the end of it. Of all people Mark blurted out, "Hey, that's not such a bad idea, Derek." He walked right up to me and took me completely by surprise as he put both his arms around me to pin my arms down so he could give me this disgustingly wet kiss on the lips—smack. (Mark's lips are *so* similar to Gloria's) Then he knocked Bob over onto Derek so that they both went tumbling into the grass together. Then he crumpled my legs with a flying body block and we all found ourselves with our appendages intertwined.

"Hey, what am I supposed to do?" complained Donnie about his state of isolation. He then quickly felt all four of us up (somewhat accurately in my case). Derek pretended to be insulted and retaliated by grabbing Donnie's crotch, pretending to punish him by yet another genital assault. Just as I was wondering which of the five of us would weaken under cross-examination at the special hearing and do us all in with the authorities, two women walking small children in strollers came into view. So we all composed ourselves and took off on the final leg of the run home.

I heard Derek drawl to Mark, "I'm glad to see you and Casey back together again."

"Hush, wench," said Mark in a decidedly uncharacteristically mock-effeminate fashion. But his eyes sparkled and he was smiling. He put his arms around Derek and me and all the guys followed suit for a few seconds. Then I picked up my frisbee and we started passing it to each other for the final phase of our run. Now if high school could always be so much fun.

However, in musing over this, I must say that while my attitude towards guys is somewhat changing, I got nervous out there because HOMOSEXUALITY in HIGH SCHOOL spells TROUBLE. If any of these guys talk to the "wrong" people about it, it could be more than embarrassing. I guess the fooling around was okay, though, just fairly typical of locker-room stuff as long as it didn't get "out of hand." Even uptight straight guys like Tom get into this stuff. I guess it's no big deal.

I'm still surprised by Mark, though. His silliness was still so affectionate—all the barriers were momentarily down. As for Derek, Bob, and Donnie, maybe there's more of this stuff around than I know about.

May 22, 1990

CASEY'S DREAM

Casey couldn't believe graduation was only three weeks away, yet the days at school seemed to pass by so slowly that he also sometimes felt high school was going to last forever. The Saturday seminars at Columbia managed to keep things perking somewhat inside his prematurely wasted mind and sharing the course with Gloria and Rob was a gas.

Dr. Bronstein encouraged them to get familiar with how the unconscious mind worked, how it could be influenced by indirect suggestion and symbols and how their dreams, if they could remember them, could provide their conscious minds with useful clues for what was happening in their lives. He said he tried to be very careful to avoid definite interpretations because he wanted each one of them on his or her own to familiarize themselves with their own inner workings.

One Sunday morning Casey woke up sensing how this phase of his life in Hastings was coming to a close. Dad and Sally had been talking about possibly selling the house once Becky graduated from high school in two years. For no reason at all—it was a warm, beautiful May morning with all kinds of beautiful scents in the air—he just started crying and crying.

After about ten minutes of crying, Casey suddenly remembered a dream from the previous night. First he saw Gloria, actually she was a mixture of Gloria and Sally, but mainly Gloria. This woman knew he was sad and opened her arms to allow him to bury his face in her midsection. He felt so vulnerable, but so protected. It was like a vision of Gloria in the future, a Gloria who totally understood his feelings better than he did himself. Did she represent his own anima?

A fade-out to another scene. He was still feeling stripped down to these raw feelings. Then he saw a male figure whose eyes were calm and full of understanding. Was it Rob? Casey held back from putting his arms around him, for he didn't think it was possible to repeat what he had just experienced with the woman.

Slowly, Casey approached the male figure, his eyes turned away. Then Casey positioned his body next to the man and then put his arm tentatively around his waist, took it away, and backed away once again. What the male figure said surprised Casey, "You don't have to leave Mark behind."

Suddenly Casey's dream mood changed. He felt filled with joy as he realized, "So Pat was right; sacrifices aren't really necessary." He started crying in his sleep, really bawling his head off. Finally he woke up, puzzled as to whether he had actually been crying or not—until he felt the moisture in his eyes and on his cheeks.

Later Casey felt he needed to tell Sally about the dream. Her energy was just what he needed. But at breakfast he just couldn't do it. He wanted the experience as his very own. By the time he kissed her good-bye and ran out to play frisbee, he was actually feeling pretty good.

PART IV

COTUIT, 1990

Monday, June 18, 1990, Cotuit, MA.

Suddenly it's the middle of June. I'm back at the Cape, working at Beck's Boatworks as a clerk in the retail sales office. It's an okay job because I get to be alone a lot, and I'm saving some money for school. Nothing much is happening now, anyway. Gloria's still home with Val, and Mark's just about to take off for New Mexico to a commune where some of Val's old friends have settled in Santa Fe. He'll use that as his base of operations for hitchhiking around the West. Of course he wants to go back packing, mountain-climbing, wind-sailing, hang-gliding, white-water rafting, surfing, and everything else. Gloria and I plan to meet him out there in August. Mom and Herb have offered the Mill Valley house for our rendezvous.

How can I fill in the missing weeks here? Graduation with all its rituals came and went. I'm glad it's over. Funny, but for some reason I got into studying during the last month when a lot of the others were goofing off, so I ended up getting all A's and high Regents scores. My teachers all seemed to give me the benefit of the doubt at the end too; I even got a couple of A+'s! I almost never admit it to *any-body*, but I get a kick out of getting good grades. At least I don't feel so intellectually inferior around real brains like Gloria and Rob.

At the graduation dance, so many people came up to me, most of them bombed out of their minds, and told me how much they liked me and how much I had cheered them up on some of their gray days with my silly antics in class. Even Joe approached me, pretty drunk, but acting real nice. He put his arm around me and started reminiscing about some of our wild times. Finally, he said, "I hope you'll stay in touch. Send me your address and phone number. Don't forget your old pals altogether once you're out there."

And Dr. Pompious came up to me, also pretty drunk. Making sure no one could overhear him, even though the band's level was ear-splitting, he practically yelled into my ear, "You know, Casey, I was terribly down on you at first last fall because I thought your wisecracks were full of sexual innuendoes suggesting I was gay. I'm sorry. Over the years I've become paranoid. It was all my projection."

"It's not paranoia when something like Pamela's outburst happens."

"Thanks, Casey. You definitely helped me then. To my way of thinking, you may not have been a perfect composition student, but you've proved yourself a good person. My only worry is that you won't work hard enough on your studies next year. You seem to have the knack down of doing the minimum to get good grades. That's a dubious quality when you're going to college."

I laughed and told him not to worry. But, you know, he had been so open and trusting, I actually took his advice in certain sense. I'm going to work hard, but be really efficient so I can still have lots of fun.

Enough retrospective. My first adventure out here resulted from Pat's visit last weekend. I told him I was interested in finding out more about his friendship with Dad.

"Pat, can I read your journal from last year? Do you know I accidentally walked into Dad's bedroom last summer when you were holding him like a little kid?"

"That's amazing, amazing that you, the Wonder-Teen would just happen upon us at a unique point in our friendship. Chuck was troubled about some legal matters that day and I convinced him to...Hey, wait a minute. I *will* let you read it. I've brought it with me because every year at the beginning of summer vacation I reread the previous year's journal."

"Pat, do you still have your journal from college? Would you let me read a couple of sections about Dad?"

"Wow, Casey. That's kinda heavy...I guess you can. Why not? Except I'm afraid you'll take some things the wrong way."

Pat looked down as he tried to figure out how I'd react to his journal. "You must remember I was sometimes flip or cynical in those days. There were so many bummers then." Then he paused and stared into space for a few seconds. "You must promise me just one thing. Ask questions about anything you don't totally understand. No guesswork, please. I'll dig out and mark some appropriate excerpts when I get home. Meanwhile, you can read last summer's.

I read it yesterday. Here's the one section I just had to transcribe.

June 10, 1989

Once again the inevitable return to the Cape. Both Eddie and I are appreciating having some space away from each other. Also, there's already a bonus of sorts. Chuck really opened up with me this weekend, and I think that had a good deal to do with Eddie's not being here.

What happened, simply, was that Chuck was totally exhausted from a couple of very sticky, trying cases he's involved with right now, especially that one with the lesbian mother. He was, in fact, weary to the point of incipient illness, so that he was reduced to quietly resting in his bedroom. After I brought him in a pot of tea, I suggested that he rest all day, that he not do anything except try to imagine floating, just drifting like a cloud in the sky. That's difficult for him as he's still a workaholic, still more or less driven, but at this point more out of habit than a need to prove himself.

We just lay together for half an hour, not saying a word. I started thinking about our friendship over the years. Maybe he was too. Ever since turning forty I've become more detached about all my friendships with straight men. At times I've felt the potential so strongly with so many of them.

But I have to handle the disappointing results. Chuck's the prototype for me, here. I've never given up hoping that we'll return to something like the wonderful active affection we shared in college. Sex, I still insist, is not a key issue, although I'd prefer our kind of friendship to have some component of physical affection, so that there would be an easygoing sense of shared warmth.

Yesterday he escaped from that hard-working, family-man identity for a couple of hours, more out of need than desire, I suspect. We said very little—that's what made it work. Instead, he reached his arms out to me at one point and we hugged, "letting go" in a way that felt good after so many years. Then he gradually allowed me to help "re-charge" him. At one point, he was actually letting me hold him like a baby. A sense of possibility seemed to be in the air, but nothing else transpired. We dozed for a bit, then I left while he was still asleep.

Later, he did look better, but already I could sense that he had come to regard the episode as an unusual occurrence. He was returning to his usual self. His typically bland facial expression returned, with that slightly furrowed brow that fits in so well with his salt and pepper, graying hair.

Chuck makes so many things possible for his clients and the members of his family. It's beautiful in its own way. He's certainly no longer the hero-idol-saviour I imagined him to be at college, but neither has living with Eddie totally erased those old feelings of love I have for him. Luckily, my life is already fine, regardless of how I get along with unpredictable friends like Chuck.

Sunday, June 24, 1990

A lot of interesting stuff happened this weekend. After I spent a quiet week of working and reading, Gloria came up for a long weekend, and we had an absolutely great time on Friday night—absence certainly does seem to make the heart grow fonder. Then Pat came down on Saturday, once again without Eddie, but with his college journal.

We had an interesting talk. He told me that he found the freedom Gloria and I give to each other to be remarkable.

Afterwards I read Pat's journal from college and it was a powerful experience. I've extracted a few key passages.

February 19, 1961

Last night was no doubt one of the happiest and most memorable of my life. All the potential I saw in my friendship with Chuck came to fruition. For once neither of us had any meetings or rehearsals. Jon was away so that we knew we had the whole suite to ourselves. There was some cognac and we got all fuzzy and warm together in Chuck's bedroom. Stretched out on his bed, we had a long hug and then Chuck uttered the magic words, "I hope you'll sleep with me in here tonight." It was a clear-cut invitation that somehow made all the frustration and restraint of the last couple of years meaningful.

I hardly have to write in here what I will always remember anyway. Enough to say that we *did* sleep together, that we *were* sexual. Chuck had more sexual curiosity and initiative than I would have thought possible—life holds its pleasant surprises. Needless to say it was wonderful to touch the friend with whom I have so long wanted to be intimate on all levels—emotionally and sexually as well as intellectually.

I have such a warm afterglow. I don't know what the future holds, but maybe, just maybe, this final undergraduate semester will be a totally happy one.

March 7, 1961

I'm forced to admit that Chuck does not want to continue our romance. In truth, I knew this from the second time we slept together, just a few days after that wonderful first night. Instead of remaining spontaneous, we've fallen into roles. Chuck's sexual curiosity or whatever seems to have run its course. Or to put it crassly, he was still willing to accept oral stimulation, but wasn't interested in that kind of deep, emotional sharing we had the first time. The whole interaction started becoming one-dimensional and mechanical. I felt outraged, used, even. Part of me was still desperate enough so that *any* physical contact was better than none at all, but so much of me automatically turned off. He was just going through the motions instead of confronting the issue and saying openly to me, "No more. I can't accept this side of myself. I refuse to deal with it." I think he knows unconsciously that his chilly behavior will eventually cause me to stop seeking sex with him, but I still think he's being a moral coward by not talking to me about how his feelings for me have changed.

Once again, even in this supposedly cosmopolitan culture here, I am without a sexual partner. If Chuck offered himself again, I'd find it hard to turn him down when there's nothing in its place. Or is it time to finally hit the streets? I have turned twenty-one, after all, but no, not the bars. That looking-glass world is torture to me. But where can I go instead?

April 29, 1961

It's no good with Chuck. All pretenses of a romantic relationship have completely disappeared. We haven't even spent a minute alone together since before spring break. *C'est fini.*

Yes, we will always stay friends; I know I should be grateful for that. And he was more open to me than 99.9% of all adult, heterosexual males. But I am *queer*. In the future I guess it'll be masochistic for me to relate romantically to any man who has not firmly declared, "I am homosexual."

But where can I go? I hate those secretive bars in Boston. And those piss-elegant, pseudo-cultural salons are populated by creatures from another planet as far as I'm concerned. I always end up bolting out in disgust, even though I accept the invitations out of desperation, hoping to find a fellow alienated student rather than those limp-wristed, affected stereotypes bitching away at one another.

Are there any other choices? I'm so restless. I've been going to the gym twice a day just to see naked men. Six more weeks of college, with a lot of work to do on my senior thesis. But there's also a sense of freedom in the air. I feel free to stay up all night, to do anything I want, but what is there? Cruising around at two or three in the morning is only initially exciting. I know there are some other men like me out there in the night, but I just can't handle cruising very well. Besides, I rarely ever see a man cruising who I'm strongly attracted to.

Am I old-fashioned? I mean it all sounds like a prescription for frustration. Aren't there any other men who feel like me? Well, I'm convinced I can't find them in those certain bathrooms on campus. It's the same as cruising the streets. The men just aren't at all appealing. That's why I was so hopeful about Chuck. We had such a fine thing going. But here I am, lonely and frustrated once again, with no possible course of action to alleviate the situation. I find it more and more easy to understand why some people attempt suicide.

* * *

Whew. Heavy stuff. I felt so sorry for Pat I started to cry. In other entries I found out he dated quite a bit at college, and some of his accounts of the times he had are pretty funny. I guess that's what he meant by his glib, cynical side; he could really be kind of cruel and sexist when he wanted to be. And there were accounts of his going out on double-dates with Dad and Mom. His perspective on their relationship over the months before they married is illuminating. He actually predicted that the marriage would collapse, that Dad's compulsiveness would only cause Mom to become more desperately needy and eventually drive her to some kind of emotional crisis.

What really hit home while I read about Pat and Dad was how much my own feelings are like Dad's. That's why I'm being so careful with Rob. I don't want to let him down. Shit, this world sucks, I swear it does. If I wasn't so confused myself and if I had any guts, I'd be able to completely accept all the various sides of me.

But my life would be very different if I accepted my attraction to men. I'm not Chuck. If I start a relationship with a man, I'm not going to run away from it right away.

But goddammit, maybe I will go ahead with it. Dammit, when Chuck comes up here for a while in a couple of weeks, I'm not going to let him run away before he answers some of my questions.

Saturday, July 7, 1990

THE BIG CONFRONTATION

Casey was determined to cause some kind of trouble when he cornered his father in Chuck's bedroom. Chuck had just made the tedious six hour drive from New York City and was, no doubt, exhausted. This fact registered itself in Casey's consciousness, but only for a split second. Instead his anger intensified when he flashed upon how unavailable Chuck had recently been because of his work.

"I want to talk to you *now*," Casey almost sneered. He wanted the drama this very instant, and if Chuck were cranky and irritable, so much the better. Let the sparks fly. Let the shit hit the fan.

"You know," said Casey, sounding condescending and appearing very upset, "You know I cannot truly respect you as a human being. Your politics are great, your humanitarian spirit is fine, but I think you're spineless where it most counts—you don't *live* your ideas out."

"C'mon Casey, I know you've been reading Pat's journals, and I'm happy he has such a positive influence on you (remember I allowed him to influence you, dear one), but you've got to leave me alone on the male-intimacy thing. I mean it's a fringe area, just for a few. Haven't I always said that it's okay with me if..."

"Yeah, yeah, 'it's okay if you, son, want to love men,' " said Casey, trying to mimic Chuck, " 'but *I* simply don't have the time in my life—my clients, my family, my need to be alone.' Yeah, yeah, I know. But I don't respect you all that much for that attitude. I mean *every* parent should allow a child to find himself. You're just guilty about letting down Pat and so you've tried to make it up by giving extra permission to me to be closer to men!"

Chuck looked annoyed, but he was silent for a few moments. "Casey, I see that you're angry at me, but I'm not sure what it's all about. If you want to be different from me, go ahead. Do it, it's okay with me. Just remember to be careful out there, because a lot of people will give you a rough time about it."

Casey got even more incensed at what he thought was his father's implication that he might not be able to handle negative reactions to his behavior.

"Come off it, Dad. *You're* the one who's afraid of public opinion, who kept telling us to watch ourselves at school and around town when you were on the Board."

"That was just politics. I thought you'd like being in on my plans to reform the Hastings schools. Leave me alone, now. I'm too tired to argue."

"I *still* say you don't live your ideas out."

"Casey, you're starting to get me very angry. Don't you remember all the time I took to sit down with you and explain controversial issues? Remember when we both listened to those homophobic cassettes by Richard Pryor and Eddie Murphy back when you were in seventh grade—a very impressionable age. And you even admitted to me you were starting to become anti-gay then, like all your friends. And remember when you insisted on seeing that God-awful Dirty Harry movie—what was its name?—the one about the woman who avenged herself on a gang of rapists by shooting off their genitals before killing them. That movie stood for everything I was against. My firm has defended thousands of women over the years—women who have been raped, some by their fathers, others who have been physically abused and mutilated, and never once did I hear of a single one who reacted the way the woman in *Sudden Impact* did—that's its name, I remember it all now, how you *insisted* on seeing it. So I let you go, on the agreement we'd talk about it afterwards. And you admitted that it truly scared the shit out of you. How many hundreds of hours did I take to do stuff like that with you?"

"But what about *living* the ideas out?" Casey refused to drop his point. "What happened to your feelings of attraction for men? Are you one of those married guys who goes to the public restrooms on the interstates to suck guys off? Do you try to seduce hitchhikers, too? Or are you just really good at control?"

"C'mon," Chuck paused, then looked exasperated. "I'm a lawyer. I couldn't take such chances. If you must know, I am still occasionally turned on by men. But I just let the feelings come and go. No big deal."

Something in Casey was first flabbergasted, then secretly delighted by the admission.

"Oh, yes!" Chuck's eyes lit up as he remembered something else he regarded as crucial to their discussion. "Look, Casey, I can specifically recall teaching you about Kinsey's heterosexual-homosexual continuum, about how we're all in different places on the scale, zero if you are totally heterosexual, six if you're exclusively homosexual. That study is *still* the accepted authority on the subject. Remember how I told you that you had to end up somewhere between zero and six, that it was fine with me wherever you ended up on the scale."

The answer momentarily satisfied some need in Casey, to make his father defend himself so vigorously. Then suddenly Casey's intuition pulled him up out of his anger as he heard an inner voice say to him, "You're both missing the point."

Suddenly illuminated, Casey blurted out without thinking, "How come you've never tried therapy. You know, when you're not around, we spend a good bit of time around here discussing your considerable hangups."

"Okay, Casey. I'll grant you that we all could benefit from some good therapy, but, you know, when your mother had her bit of a breakdown, I needed to work all the harder for a while. At the time I admitted to myself that I could use some time in therapy myself, because I knew I wasn't always on top of what I was feeling."

"What an understatement," Casey even shocked himself as his words came pouring out. "Don't you realize how legendary your emotional escapism is around here. 'Poor Chuck, his compulsive work-ethic never gives him time to deal with his feelings.' "

The light in Casey's mind suddenly brightened. He suddenly knew what he had wanted to say all along. So sure was he of his point that his anger dissolved and his usual good-natured self started to return. "Dad, I don't mean that you haven't shown us a lot of love; you've been a great father to us. I mean I know I'm lucky, *but* here's my point. You think of bisexuality only as a willingness to enjoy physically both girls and boys, vaginas and penises. But that's just the technical definition. You miss the point."

Casey paused. Chuck said nothing, but seemed attentive and possibly receptive, so Casey continued.

"Dad, the idea is that if a guy gives up trying so hard to be exclusively heterosexual, there's a change in personality that's involved—one that I think you've been avoiding. It's hard to explain it without sounding corny. What happens is that you can *relax* your whole being. You can let down your guard, you can lose control and let others initiate sometimes, you can enjoy submitting. And you don't have to care if anyone makes fun of you for being gentle or feminine or whatever, because you know yourself and *like* what you're becoming. That's the kind of man Gloria wants me to become, the kind that Rob needs, the kind Mark really is, but can't quite let himself become."

"Yes, yes, Casey. I suppose you have a point and I'm glad you're into it....Look at my life, though. You can't say I'm not used to being laughed at or attacked."

"See, Dad. You have to assert yourself to me, justifying yourself as a sacrifice for unpopular causes, but unable to just receive my ideas. The process I'm talking about is more than playing the role of a civil libertarian, although I'm not at all putting that down. It's *being*, living for joy, sharing feelings, interacting as equals as much as you possibly can."

"And this is what you're trying to do?"

"Yes, I think so. I'm still scared of being emotionally close to men, just like you, but I'm trying to see what will happen if I let my intuition guide me. I'm making mistakes and will probably make more."

"Well, maybe therapy isn't such a bad idea."

"Sure, Dad. Get yourself a good Jungian analyst, maybe a woman—anyone you feel really comfortable with. You can dig up the bucks. Indulge yourself. Get out of the sacrificing father role. You know, I'm saving you plenty from your original plans to send me to the Ivy League. And I'm going to work and get some loans too. Give me a chance to be helpful to you, materially. Give me a chance to grow up and feel self-sufficient."

"Casey, stop it. You know how important it is for me to put you through college. You're some guy, though. Try not to be so hard on your Dad just because I'm not yet ready for all your ideas. Come over here and give me a hug."

Casey felt so much relief as he willingly embraced his Dad. Never before had he felt such clear permission to become his own man.

The next evening, in the den after dinner, Chuck got off into his slightly sentimental side. "Casey, you know we don't measure you by standard parental expectations. I love you as you are—so much quick, bright, sensitive, loving intelligence. And I swear I'm happy you're self-confident enough to enter college in 1990 without having to be obsessed by a game-plan for your career. I'm happy you haven't overburdened yourself with responsibilities at school. It's that sunshine-kid smile that means so much to me." Chuck looked into Casey's eyes and realized he had made a speech. He didn't care. He just beamed at Casey.

Casey looked back at Chuck standing across from him. His anger was gone. He could hardly wait to join both Sally and Chuck for the reassuringly familiar family reunion, with some good wine and then a start-of-the-weekend dinner. And Gloria was coming tomorrow!

Monday, July 9, 1990

My euphoric mood after the Great Confrontation with Chuck did not last past that particular Friday evening. The next day I felt terrible—weak, no energy, feverish. Life moves on, the mind lags behind, as they say. At breakfast, I felt guilty for pulling a "power-trip" on Chuck. Luckily, he had gone along with my ideas to a great extent. Now I faced the pressure of keeping my word about what I had said to him about living out my ideas, for he had become a witness to the part of me that wants to get free of my own male bullshit.

Unfortunately, when Gloria showed up Saturday afternoon, I was not able to improve my mood. I explained to her what happened and she understood. "Don't feel you always have to be sky-high when you're around me, Casey. That's one of the problems I have with you, one of the reasons I do need space from you. You don't have to be so intense all the time."

At first, her words hit me like a slap in the face. While I was in that mood, some part of me, the guilty part I guess, needed to be put down, so here was the punishment I craved. So she thought I was too hyper, too artificially high! What did she know? She's the one in our relationship, it seems to me, who's always searching for bummers. Why was she picking on me when I was down? So we bickered for a while, exchanging all the other complaints we had stored up "lately" about each other.

But I couldn't go on arguing like that for very long. I felt too shitty, too much as if I were sick or something. So I just curled up into a ball, dropping my head into Gloria's lap, as if I were a pathetic invalid or something. She said nothing, but apparently liked my acting like a baby because soon I felt all this love and warmth coming from her. I think I even dozed off for a few minutes, sort of a brief return to the womb.

When I awoke, Gloria smiled at me. I felt better and my sense of confusion had passed. I no longer had that aching, gnawing inner accusation that I was crazy for trying to do something that must be "wrong." I thought of Gloria's loyalty to her own gender, and how much I respected her for it. So it logically followed she'd respect me more for my trying to improve things with guys.

So without my having to tell her, she knew, somehow, about what had recently happened to me. It felt good to get that kind of respect from Gloria, let me tell you!

It turned out to be a great evening. Very little talking. Sometimes she'd hold me; sometimes we just lay down, hugging each other. Waves of loving energy passed back and forth between us. I felt secure. Life's adventures were ahead of me and yet here was this wonderful woman to encourage me on to further adventures, just as she could count on my supporting her in the same way!

Gloria, you are totally wonderful. I love you so much. I'm so happy, so thankful that we have discovered each other.

Monday, July 16, 1990

EDDIE'S VISIT

Right from the start it was an unusual weekend because Eddie was visiting without Pat. Pat had to stay in Boston for a conference, but it also seemed to Casey that Pat and Eddie, like Gloria and himself, were emphasizing independence in their relationship these days. Casey really liked Eddie who was close to him in size and build, about six feet one, 160 pounds or so, though he had reddish-blond hair and some freckles rather than Casey's dirty blond hair and somewhat darker complexion. Eddie's extremely clear eyes were a deep blue.

With Gloria back in Boston again, it seemed like a good opportunity for Casey to get to know Eddie better, so he invited him up to the loft for a drink. Casey was a bit ill at ease because he wasn't sure what he wanted from Eddie that evening. Still, wasn't losing some control part of the process? Somewhat sleepy, he soon found himself leaning against Eddie's shoulder, which felt great, as if it were filled with a ray of light.

Casey still felt defensive because he wasn't quite back to his usual "high" mood (the one Gloria had complained about.) He muttered something apologetic to Eddie for the way he felt, but Eddie just smiled and said nothing. Then Casey remembered the word "attractive" which Pat had once used to describe him at that family dinner a few years back. Eddie, too, sure has known me for a long time, thought Casey. Hell, he's like family. I totally trust him and want him to hang around up here tonight with me.

So they smoked some weed and got zonked. Then Casey gave in to an urge and asked if Eddie wanted to sleep next to him up in the loft. Eddie agreed, they undressed, and they lay down on their backs, side by side. Soon they were floating in space together, half awake and half asleep. Then Eddie rolled over and Casey held him for a while. Casey started getting aroused when he pressed in against Eddie's backside. Then they reversed positions, and Casey could feel that Eddie was also hard. When Eddie put his hand on Casey's stomach, Casey could sense that ray-of-light effect emitting from Eddie's fingers.

Lying there being snuggled by Eddie, Casey admitted to himself that he wanted Eddie to move that light-filled hand down to his penis. He wanted to feel his cock surrounded by that electrical sense of well-being. But Eddie was being very cautious, insisting that Casey initiate, probably because he didn't want Casey to think him pushy.

Casey stretched himself out as far as he could and twisted his body slightly around so that his cock bumped into Eddie's hand. Eddie just let it lay against his hand for the longest while, then gently brushed Casey's balls with the back side of his hand. Casey snuggled in against Eddie's front and allowed Eddie to hold him tightly.

Just about then, apparently, both of them fell asleep. During the night they changed positions again and Casey held Eddie's penis as he pressed his own against Eddie's behind. Then once again they shifted, this time Eddie played a bit with Casey's cock, then whispered, "Is everything okay?"

Casey answered, "Yes," not just out of politeness. Part of him wanted to go further, but Eddie wasn't going to take the lead and he guessed he wasn't ready himself, since he wasn't doing anything, even though it was obvious Eddie wouldn't mind. He somehow needed to keep it all low-key.

In the morning, Casey discovered that he felt renewed, in a much better mood than the previous day. He kept wanting to make contact by putting his arm around Eddie's shoulders. Then Pat called and said he was fleeing the conference and would be down for Saturday night dinner after all. Casey felt somewhat relieved by the news since he wasn't yet up to trying to have a similar experience with Eddie two nights in a row and now he didn't need an excuse, although Casey knew that he really didn't need one.

He wanted time to think. For one thing Eddie and he had really connected, no denying that.

The warmth was as strong as he usually felt with Gloria. There had been no pressure, no sense of having to do anything, either.

Later that evening, the moment Pat stepped into the house to greet whoever was around, Casey was jolted by another surprise. He could swear Pat looked so young, his smiling face as radiant with energy as Mark's ever was. Pat was a beautiful man—trim, energetic, glowing with vitality.

And then a qualm of guilt hit Casey, guilt about spending the previous evening with Eddie. No, not the guilt that he had muscled in on Pat's boyfriend. He knew they both were more or less beyond that sort of thing. No, it was guilt for not having first had a similar experience with Pat. Wasn't it Pat that he had initially wanted to be that close to? Yes, it was, thought Casey, but I never would have known that if I hadn't been with Eddie first. Last night had been some kind of initiation, the result of which enabled him for the first time in his life to sense Pat not as someone he idolized, but as an equal.

Thursday, July 19, 1990

What a rough week it's been. I've been really sick, some kind of flu, with a high fever, sore throat, nausea, and a total lack of energy. God, I'd sleep all day, get the shivers, then wake up sweating. At one time when my fever was up between 104 and 105 degrees, I'd start having all this ridiculous fear about dying.

And the dreams I had. I wish I could remember them. I was usually on some difficult journey or in some situation where I was very frightened. Sweat, sweat, and more sweat.

To make matters worse, the weather was very hot and humid, the best beach weather of the summer. I felt so bummed out to be missing it. I was down on myself, too. I felt as if I hadn't done enough for myself in life, that I was too dependent on others. I was especially guilty about Sally's nursing me so much and my not giving her anything back.

At times, I'd feel ashamed of being attracted to men and kept thinking of what Tom and Joe and all those guys at school would say. "Cocksucker" is their favorite negative word.

About the fourth day I was sick, I came to the simple conclusion that the significant thing about the night with Eddie was that it *wasn't* wrong, *couldn't* be wrong in any way. It wasn't something we did out of the excitement of doing something that's supposedly forbidden. We were simply expressing affection for each other.

Gloria feels my illness came from my old, male high school self that freaked out and, in one lingering burst of negativity, got me sick. "Just look at this week as a purification, Casey. It's a rite of passage. I'm sure it's very scary trying to change."

Yup. I'm sure Gloria hit the nail on the head. That's the scary part—I need to continue to take responsibility. All of my regressions will be obvious to Gloria, even to Chuck. (Speaking of regressions, Buzz has now become a tough-guy cat with a huge gut and rippling flanks, someone who doesn't get pushed around any more. And so goes life in the food chain.)

Today, I do feel purified, but I'm suspicious of how long that sense will last. Rob's coming up to visit next week. Maybe I ought to try to talk with him more about what I'm going through. I need to find out more about his feelings for me, too.

Thursday, July 26, 1990

SETTING THE RECORD STRAIGHT

Despite not having seen Rob much since their springtime trip, Casey barely looked forward to his visit. He hadn't really missed him. In fact a part of Casey felt he *still* needed space from Rob. The entire week before his arrival, Casey found himself resenting Rob's affection, probably because he couldn't yet return it. How could the visit not be disappointing to Rob, he reasoned.

When Rob arrived, Casey immediately lost his irritability and intuitively felt that everything was falling into place. They decided on sleeping next to one another in the loft as they had done the previous summer. It had become an enjoyably acceptable ritual.

Rob was very happy about his future. If nothing else he'd get out of New York and far, far away from his parents. He even smiled mischievously upon indicating that he couldn't afford to go home to see his parents until next June. His new-found happiness definitely helped pick up Casey's spirits.

Knowing Rob was going to drive back with Chuck later that Sunday afternoon, Casey took the family skiff and sailed them across the channel to the island where they could be by themselves. Sheltered from the breeze in his favorite sand dune, Casey knew *now* was the perfect time and place for them to break their silence about some heavy matters.

"Rob, uh, I feel awkward about bringing up some of this stuff, but, uh, I want to explain why I'm, well kinda weird this weekend."

"That's okay, Casey. I can see you're going through something. I can handle it." Rob sort of forced a little laugh.

"Well, I'm trying to be mellow enough to let myself get closer to men and not worry about what it means. But it's hard with you, Rob. I mean—well, you know a lot about Gloria and me, and even though you know about us, you seem, well, oh it's so hard to say, you seem to think that there's another side of me that could really be into guys. I take it back. That's not what I mean. I want to know more about your feelings towards me. I'm kind of scared of them."

An awkward pause followed, at least it was awkward for Casey. "Casey, I bet you're afraid I've fallen hopelessly in love with you. God, that was hard for me to say." Rob heaved a deep sigh of relief.

"It sounds so silly to hear you say it," Casey replied, "but, yes, I'm afraid of the responsibility. I'm afraid I'll disappoint you, not be what you want me to be. But another part of me senses—just barely as of now—that you can love me for what I am and that you can accept me for what I am—whatever that is."

"Exactly, Casey, I am in love with you *and* I've accepted your commitment to Gloria. You know, talking to Chuck really helped me there. He never tried to shield you from my love. He never has explicitly said it to me, but he has definitely helped me feel good about my wanting to know you better."

Rob's words of praise about Chuck rankled Casey. But he caught himself this time. Jealousy—he had some petty jealousy about Chuck's taking the energy to be close to Rob, energy Casey had wanted for himself. His jealousy *was* so petty in the light of how much Rob needed a positive father-image and how much Chuck had helped Rob.

Casey's consciousness suddenly shoved the issue of jealousy aside to check out how Rob was reacting. Rob was staring at the Cotuit harbor, content to absorb the sun while Casey pondered their exchange. It felt good to Casey, so good he decided he now knew all he needed to know about Rob's feelings for him.

"You know, thanks to your Dad, I have the self-respect not to go out on dates with women anymore just to please my parents. They don't actually know I'm gay yet, but I'm going to tell them once I'm established at college. Finally, senior year, I got up enough courage to make passes at a couple of my boyfriends at school. Nothing much developed, but at least I had some good times and got some experience." Rob beamed, then looked up to Casey to reinforce the validity of his sensual highs. When Casey couldn't think of anything to say, Rob added, "At least I'm not so filled with romantic longings anymore or so desperate for *my* kind of sexual experience."

Casey could listen between the lines. Rob was saying that he no longer brought those longings to their friendship. That was a great relief. Wasn't it weird that two people who liked each other as much as he and Rob still had to work through so many issues just to become close friends? He moved over to Rob and held his hand for a few seconds. "Well, partner, time to sail back to the ranch for Sunday dinner."

"A little grub would do me just fine." Rob stood up first and helped Casey up with the arm of the hand Casey was holding. As soon as they were both standing, they put their arms around each other and gave each other an embrace. Then off they trotted back to the skiff, hoping they weren't late for dinner.

Tuesday, August 7, 1990

This last week I've been all alone with Dad. Sally's off staying with the woman she's had sort of a crush on all these years, Emilie, who's visiting for a few weeks from France. She's renting the Hodgkin's other house, so they'll be able see as much of each other as they want to. Gloria's up in Boston with her friends; she's also visiting Becky, who's at the Conservatory. She picked a good week to avoid the Cape. It's been cloudy or rainy just about the whole time.

Dad was supposed to work this week, but when Sunday night rolled around, he was just too sick to leave. (It's funny he picked the week of Emilie's return to the States to get sick. Men can certainly get threatened easily.) He looked awful too. He had a sore throat and fever, so he probably caught the same bug which got me a few weeks ago. His illness, though, has probably been the best thing that has ever happened to our relationship. I decided it was my chance to take care of him!

So I told him to relax, that I would try to be everything for him that Sally would be if she were here. His face went into a sour little smile, and he squinted skeptically at me. "Oh sure, Florence Nightingale in person. Well, I think I can manage to do okay on my own. Maybe you could just pick up a few things from the store, fruit juices and broth, maybe."

"Of course, Dad. I'll play any kind of music you want on the stereo, and I'll cook and tidy up. Oh yes, and take your temperature."

"Well, just don't be noisy. No music please. My head is pounding."

"Don't worry, Dad. I'll be out of the house most of the time. I'll check in several times a day, though."

That virus proved to be very tough on Dad. He kept throwing up any food he ate and he slept poorly at night. About the third day, he was so weak and pathetic that he actually let me pamper him. So I started having some fun fluffing up his pillow, giving him massages, even climbing in bed with him and holding him for a while, despite his protests that I might get sick again.

Once, looking directly into his face while lying next to him in the dim, late-morning light of a drizzly morning, I noticed the gray in his three-day beard as well as in his hair. His face was droopy and pasty, but he was softer, more lovable, mortal in a way that at first frightened me. He was my Dad, the provider, after all! Then I relaxed, felt a sudden surge of love, and hugged him.

"Whatever it is you're becoming, Casey, it's pretty wonderful. You sure make your old, sick Dad feel proud.

"This illness is ridiculous," Chuck continued. "I must have been almost totally exhausted to get this sick. And, yet, I've barely missed Sally, and I've been totally content to be here with you. I feel we're becoming friends, a good thing too because I'm no longer quite the same old dad for you I used to be. Well, you'll be off for good in a couple of weeks. I'm glad all this happened before you left."

Casey felt good after hearing those words. He wanted to return Chuck's gift. "Just promise me, Dad, while I'm gone you'll work less and give yourself more time to have fun."

"I promise. I'm going to delegate more responsibility at work and concentrate only on the crucial cases."

"Sounds great, Dad."

"Hey, there's good old Buzz. He's been snuggling with me all week. How's he been? I haven't seen him with any abscesses this summer."

"Nope, not yet. On his second birthday, I told him to fight only when it was absolutely necessary to establish his territory. And that if he does fight, he shouldn't get hurt."

"And it worked?"

"More or less. He still gets beat up a little every now and then, but no major wounds. But, you know, you never see strange cats around any more. I'm grateful we men don't have to live like tom cats, that constant fighting and competition—yuck."

"Wise words. I'll be one happy guy if I can retire before I'm an old, battered alley cat."

Wednesday, August 8, 1990

Mill Valley, CA
July 31, 1990

Dear Casey,

How ya' doing, partner? Here I am in the Bay Area after spending a month or so in the Sun Belt. Sorry I haven't written or called earlier, but I've been on the move. I spent most of the first month in New Mexico, checking out some local scenes, hiking around and exploring the mountains. I moved on to Arizona and tripped on the desert until the heat got to me. Believe it or not I started missing the cool, gray, foggy nights on the Cape.

Then I hitchhiked into Southern California and spent a couple of weeks hanging around beach towns—La Jolla, Encinitas, Leucadia—they're all just north of San Diego. The swimming and weather were great, but I started feeling uptight since there's a huge percentage of people down there who have gotten together and agreed to pretend that it's still 1955 or something. So I found a ride with a couple of guys from New Jersey, of all places. They said they were driving Route 1 through Big Sur all the way to the Bay Area. So I split expenses with them and we spent four sunny days, no fog at all, taking it slowly up the coast. When I got into San Francisco, I called Danny, and he invited me to stay for a while.

Then this job came up, working with Danny. I've always liked working with wood, and he's into metal, so we got on this construction crew and made good bucks. When a couple of the regulars decided to take off for Hawaii, we were offered regular jobs, as of Labor Day or so. I'm going to start living with your Mom, paying rent, but then Danny and I are going to look for our own place out by the ocean.

I'm feeling real good about having a steady source of income. As you know, I don't want to go to college yet. I think I'll have time to work on some art stuff out here too, and, of course, I'll be within a couple hours of you and Gloria.

I want to tell you something, that I missed you an awful lot. I expected to be lonely some of the time and that was okay. But then there were other times I missed you personally so much. *I was surprised, believe me.*

Actually, that happened on the desert. I wanted to prove I could survive on my own out there for a few days. It was so beautiful—so incredibly quiet. So I started having all these imaginary conversations with you. It's hard to explain but I was actually looking at my life through your eyes.

Well, Casey, you're a tough guy for an ordinary bloke like me to compare himself with. Sometimes I was kind of pissed at you. You were the one, not me, who had held it all together, doing well in school and going to college and still keeping it fun and all that. And you're the one who has this great relationship with my sister, the only guy she's ever respected. And here I am—alone, fucked-up, wandering aimlessly around the desert.

After being pissed off for a few days, my mood

changed and I admitted to myself what I really liked about you was the way you could dig so many kinds of people. You're very good at loving people and you've been showing me how all along, very, very unobnoxiously. But I have been dense, just a space case a lot of the time.

It won't be too long before I come east to get organized for moving out here. Maybe we could come back out here together.

In any case thanks for being my main man. We'll have some wild times celebrating our move to California.

Love,
Mark

Sunday, August 12, 1990

GLORIA'S SURPRISING REVELATION

Since they all would soon be off to California, Casey sent Gloria a big, fancy invitation to spend a final night of celebration together in the loft before their imminent return to Hastings and points west. He sighed when he thought about how well things had been going lately with Gloria. Maybe they were becoming closer to help each other feel more secure during their move to new turf.

Gloria and Casey began their commemorative evening on the Cape with luscious vegetarian pizza from Neapolitan Madness after a pleasant drive over to Osterville. Casey had snuck in his sheepskin filled with red wine, so they dined as adult lovers at one of the plushy red booths at the back of the restaurant. They enjoyed every instant of eye-contact, sitting across from each other. (Am I the only guy that gets an erection from eye-action, wondered Casey?) He felt so loving, so grateful to the world-at-large that everything in their lives seem to have conspired to work for their mutual advantage. Everything just kept going well for him and *still* he hadn't been struck by lightning.

Casey was interrupted from his reveries by a question from Gloria. He asked her to repeat herself, for he thought he had heard the names Leslie and Adrienne.

"I apologize, Casey. I know this is not the best time to bring up this subject, on this romantic date together and everything. But I do want to verify—to tell you for sure I suppose—that my friends, Leslie and Adrienne, were the same women you and Mark met on the beach at the Vineyard."

"How can it be?" stammered Casey. "Don't they have steady boyfriends or something? When did you get to know them anyway? They're not your original friends, are they?" Casey started feeling somewhat uncomfortable. Why was Gloria bringing them up anyway?

"Actually, I did meet my original friends through Becky up in Boston. These other friends also go to the Conservatory during the summers and both have steady boyfriends. But, as far as I know, it's been quite a while since Adrienne and Leslie have had boyfriends, although they occasionally date, sometimes even double date. You see they're, well, what word do you use—sort of 'lovers.' Actually 'best friends' is a better description, best friends who are sometimes lovers."

"Sometimes lovers! Don't they know what they are, for heaven's sake?"

"Casey, even *you* admit your confusion. I certainly don't know how to label myself, either."

"So why are we talking about this now," said Casey, a little on edge.

"I need to be honest with you." Gloria gazed straight into his eyes with her patented no-bullshit look. "I want to tell you about a night I spent with Leslie and Adrienne on my last visit there. I had been getting more and more comfortable being physically affectionate with them, each time I saw them. So the last time I was up visiting, we decided to all three sleep together, sort of innocently, like a pajama party, only one thing led to another, and I was very curious, so I ended up having my first sexual experience with women."

Casey was stunned. He knew something like this was up for months, but his male pride balked at the cruel twist of fate that Gloria's partners were one and the same as those in his only "mature" fantasy-come-true sexual experience. Now that experience seemed somehow less significant.

Gloria seemed to know what he was thinking. "Look, Casey, don't be hurt. They're super-choosey about male partners. They truly liked you and Mark. You guys were lucky that day. So do think of it as a golden memory."

Casey was hurt. He wasn't sure why. Yes, he did know. He was jealous, jealous of Gloria's ongoing friendship with them, jealous that she didn't even have to make a choice, as he and Mark did. But then he remembered that both he and Gloria were just about to leave for California. What a relief. Maybe this kind of thing wouldn't happen again for a while. In spite of that thought, he couldn't help saying, "I suppose I better get use to your sleeping around. And I suppose the experience was much better than being with me because they didn't lay any male pressure-trips on you."

"That's low, Casey. Actually it wasn't that perfect an experience. First of all, I could feel the tension from their competing for me. I had to try to give each one of them equal attention or the other would pout. Three-ways are difficult at best, I guess. And I have to admit that I did feel used afterwards. I know they both like me, but I found them too physically aggressive, much more than you. I needed to be eased into the situation. They went too fast for me—yes, I did feel a female-pressure trip."

Casey felt better. Of course he had liked their sexual aggressiveness that sunny day on the Vineyard. No one played any games, and everyone acknowledged desiring instant gratification. But he could see Gloria's side of it too. He loved her for being so honest, even for trying so obviously to help heal his injured male ego.

"The whole thing has made me confused about where I stand with women," Gloria went on. "I need to pull back a little now and get some perspective on my feelings, although I know, one way or another, that I do want to continue to try to be closer to women. Anyway, you should know I haven't been deceiving you that much. It was only last month that we all made the connection about the Vineyard. I was hoping for all of us to have a reunion at the party next week, but it turns out they have auditions and can't make it."

"Wow, I'm still a bit flabbergasted. What's Becky's opinion of all this, anyway?"

"Casey, how nice of you to inquire about the welfare of your baby sister."

"C'mon Gloria, gimme a break."

"Okay, Becky's just fine, just taking it all in. Leslie and Adrienne are like big sisters to her. And Becky's also getting guidance from talking to Sally about her friendship with Emilie."

"Gosh, that's right. I've been timid about asking Sally about it, but also curious. It's great that

Sally's expanding her life, now that the kids are leaving. Two more years of Becky and that's it."

"Well, I can tell you everything's gone very well for Sally with Emilie. Emilie doesn't define herself as a lesbian, but she's had some experiences with women in France. Basically, they are just getting to know each other better."

"So it's not unlike Chuck and Pat, an old college friendship, updated and revised."

"Yes, except Emilie's not sure if she'll stay in the States. Still, that would give Sally an excuse to visit her in France. Sally's told me she's learned a lot from watching us kids. She and Emilie go on hikes or go sailing or they just lie around with a bottle of wine, listening to music and being cozy together. Sally can't believe how many subtle romantic overtones there are. All those years of writing letters really deepened their affection."

Casey took it all in, still somewhat jealous, but relieved to be part of a family that encouraged such explorations. Then Gloria and he lapsed into contented silence, their legs gently touching under the table. Just at the right moment, Gloria jumped up and suggested a walk at twilight on the local beach. So they strolled along the beach, holding hands, while Gloria set a brisk pace so that they wouldn't get too nostalgic about growing up and having to leave the Cape.

And then back to the loft. Actually, Gloria had been a fairly frequent visitor there lately, possibly because, like Casey, she realized that their time of easy, convenient get-togethers was almost over. Casey uncorked some California champagne. Gloria lit some candles. The world was totally soft and still, except for a summer zephyr easing its way gently up to them through the screens of the loft. They listened to space music for a while, George Winston and Jean-Michel Jarre. How wonderful it was to hold Gloria in his arms and kiss her for hours, knowing that there was no pressure, no hurry at all.

Casey felt as if he were just oozing with love for Gloria. He looked at how she wore her T-shirt. Sure, you could easily see her breasts, her nipples even, underneath. But what he really liked was the way the shirt flopped over her long, sinewy, muscular arms. The soft, faded color of the pink-red shirt seemed to bring out the deep reddish-copper of her tan. Gloria was so healthy, so comfortable with her body, so *there*. He shuddered to think how unusual she was, how lucky he was. Well, at least going to different colleges would ensure his not taking her for granted, if that were possible.

"Casey, it is so fine being up here with you. I love the way you allow things to happen, to let us warm up until we're floating in the clouds. That's how I'm feeling now. Gosh, I have given you some rough times during the past year or so, but you always show how classy you are. Casey-cakes, don't ever change. Always be the sweet guy you are now."

What could Casey say? Compliments from Gloria weren't that rare, but Casey always felt mighty good afterwards because Gloria never said anything just to be nice or to get you to like her.

So Casey, too, overflowed with love and inevitably they melted together, floating into blissfulness. Their chemistry was so powerful it mattered little now what kind of sexual activity they chose. All-American boy that he was, his penis never declined any kind of invitation from Gloria.

And now, naked together under a single sheet on that warm summer night, they alternately made love and dozed all night long, waking up refreshed. Casey felt so high at breakfast. Oh, the way Gloria looked across the table and smiled at him! How could everything else in life not be fine with a lover like her?

As he sat there enjoying a deep sense of calmness, Casey realized why the night had been so fine. Yes, it had been their last night in the loft for a long time, but there had been something else. Gloria had been unusually high, and so Casey's curiosity impelled him even on this ideal morning to ask her about why she had been so responsive.

"Oh, Casey," Gloria cooed. "There was something about you last night—you were so soft, so deep, so patient, so reassuring. You haven't been learning from someone else, have you?"

Casey laughed at what he thought was the ridiculousness of Gloria's perception. But after sitting still quietly for a minute or so, he did make a connection. Patience, reassurance, warmth? Those qualities suddenly invoked Eddie's presence. Well, well. Maybe he had learned something from Eddie after all.

Tuesday, August 14, 1990

BOYHOOD BUDDIES ONCE AGAIN

The scene once again is the loft. This time, Casey's guest is none other than Mark, who surprised the hell out of him by showing up, without his moustache, just as Casey was packing up to leave the Cape. At dinner, Mark informed everyone that it was definite that he was going out to Mill Valley to work construction.

Mark and Casey settled in among the massive, slightly musty pillows in the loft, happy to be with each other again. Casey poured each of them a rum and orange juice. Neither said much during the first drink which they both instantly guzzled. Casey poured them another. "I love this stuff. It's getting me kind of mushy, though, Mark. Your letter amazed me. You seem happier, as if you've stopped giving yourself such a hard time."

"You had a lot to do with it."

"Mark, I can't tell you how good you've been for me, too. You always know how to have fun, whatever the situation, you know what I mean? You're in touch with a great wild energy—you're the only one who can really bring it out in me."

"Thanks." Mark looked self-conscious and took a long sip on his drink.

"Hey, Mark," Casey broke the ice, returning to a less awkward subject of conversation, "Congratulations on getting a construction job out there. That's hard to do, you know. Are you going to drive west with Gloria, Rob, and me? Dad has a friend who needs a huge gas-guzzler delivered out to California, so we'll travel for free, with quite a lot of space for our junk."

"Sure, I'd love to go with you guys. It'll be fun. We can take turns driving. I know about hot springs and stuff we can stop at if we want to take our time."

"Fabulous." Casey was amazed to discover this wasn't totally a new Mark. He was back to being as he was when he was eleven or twelve, with that wild kid-playfulness, eyes sparkling like crazy.

"You know, I guess the trip made me realize that most of the stuff our families do is really okay. I will say it took a few nasty encounters with rednecks this summer to make me sure of what I *didn't* want to be like. I'll spare you the details and tell you that I'd much rather be like you."

"Mark—it's so great being back with you."

With those words, Casey jumped Mark and hugged and wrestled and rolled around with him. Mark was wearing the same kind of faded, soft, pink-red cotton T-shirt Gloria had worn two nights earlier. Those floppy clothes somehow helped make both of them super-appealing. He and Mark put their arms around each other and fell back onto the pillows. Soon they were dozing together.

When Casey woke up a bit later, he whispered, "Let's chuck our clothes." He pulled Mark to him again, and Mark rolled right into Casey's waiting arms. Then Casey pulled up the sheet and could swear they were glowing together in the dark.

He wondered about being sexual that night. He didn't really feel like it. Mark, too, seemed to be putting sex on hold; tonight's only purpose was for showing his love. Anyway, Mark and he were already tighter than ever before. That was plenty for one night.

As they lay there together, Casey figured Mark was still in transition. Give him more space, give him more time; he doesn't have to label himself just so he has something to say to people.

As Casey drifted towards sleep, his mind continued to make connections. He was so happy to not be leaving behind his boyhood pal. Why had he kept obsessing on the sexual aspects of Pat and Chuck's friendship, forgetting they were boyhood buddies too. Maybe he'd talk to them more about their childhood together before he left. Probably they had both been too paranoid to have any sex while they were still kids. And with that thought, Casey fell asleep entwined with Mark.

Monday, August 27, 1990 Mill Valley, CA.

A NEW SORT OF FEELING

Casey was exhausted. It was 4 a.m., but he was still too wired after the party to sleep. He was excited; he could hardly believe that he was in California—this time for good.

He recalled the Great Farewell Party back in Hastings. It had been Mark's presence that had stood out for him. The energy Mark put out socially—there was now a verbal, sophisticated, Val-like side of him. Poor Val got a little weepy then. Imagine losing the company of both Gloria and Mark? Still she was so happy about the changes in her son. After a couple of drinks, she started kissing Casey like crazy, slobbering all over him, thanking him for his good influence on Mark, and then there were so many hugs and good-byes.

And then they all hit the road, deciding to foresake all side trips and get to California as quickly as possible, for they wanted to take advantage of the two weeks before college to have fun in the Bay Area.

At the welcoming party the previous evening, Casey's Mom had come up to him and told him she was really impressed by Rob. "You're so lucky to have already such a great college buddy. Are you going to be roommates?"

"Nope," replied Casey. "We could, but we've decided to start off independently. We'll both be living on campus, in the same college in fact, so it'll be easy to see a lot of each other."

"And Gloria over at Stanford," Casey's Mom gave him a wink, "It shouldn't be too hard to see her. You can have study weekends together."

"Yeah. We'll both have an escape hatch when things get too hectic."

"C'mon, Casey, aren't you a little scared about Gloria's meeting all those rich, handsome, intelligent Stanford men, especially with her being pre-med and all?" Casey remained silent and smiled. "Not that I think you should worry, mind you."

"Thanks Mom, for your stirring vote of confidence in me." Another deep breath. "Actually though, I'm becoming philosophical about it all. If she meets someone else, fine. But she and I are really rolling along right now. We've already adjusted somewhat to giving each other independent lives. That's my ace in the hole. Those Stanford guys will try to possess her because they don't know any other way to approach her. Then I'll look even better to her. Hell, why not be confident and optimistic, anyway?"

"That's the spirit," Diane declared as she threw her arms around Casey and surprised him with the strength of her squeeze.

Suddenly, Gloria grabbed Casey's rear end from behind. He wheeled around, and lost himself in her eyes, but she brought him abruptly out of his daze as she said, "Oh Casey, I kind of want to sleep with you tonight, but, I mean, I know there are others here who...well, I'm ready to defer my..."

"Gloria, I'm shocked! You know you've got the inside track. Or are you looking for an excuse for some space?"

"Casey, you turd. None of that east coast irony out here in Lotus Land. Actually I am charmed by your acceptance of my offer. See you at our 'late date.' "

That Gloria! He liked her making the decisions because things were always a delightful surprise when they worked out. And then she couldn't accuse him of pressuring her.

A few minutes later, just as Casey was about to go upstairs to his rendezvous with Gloria, a somewhat schlocked Rob walked up, took him by the hand, and led him outside into the cool, sobering night air. They walked around the suburban neighborhood in the moonlight for about ten minutes, neither of them saying a word. Casey could feel surges of energy coming from Rob's hand. After a few minutes, Casey discovered he wanted Rob to touch him, to maybe even come on to him the way a guy tries to make out with a girl on his first date or something. Rob was, if anything, nicer, softer than ever before, so safely powerful in his big frame that Casey wanted to be swept up by him.

A few seconds later Rob began bumping Casey around, pretending he was a tough football pro, overwhelming Casey comically, slamming him into a wall. Casey remained "slammed" there, waiting for Rob to crush his front into Casey's. That crotch-pressure felt good at this point in the evening. Obviously, neither of them was going to speak at all.

Rob put his arms around Casey, just a trifle awkwardly, as if signalling he wanted to wrap up this little episode. Despite his size, despite that sharp analytic mind, there was something so sweet and innocent about Rob's whole approach. Besides Casey had decided he liked occasionally to be swept off his feet. And so Casey hugged Rob back, even gave him a quick little kiss on the neck. What the fuck, thought Casey, as they walked back to the house, arms around each other's shoulders.